Time-Fixer, the Beginning

Book 1 –Pleistocene Repair

By Steve Preston

2nd Edition

© Copyright 2019, Steve Preston
All rights reserved.
No part of this book may be reproduced, stored in a retrieval system, or transmitted by any means, electronic, mechanical, photocopying, recording, or otherwise, without written permission from the author.

Table of Contents

TIME-FIXER, THE BEGINNING	1
TABLE OF CONTENTS	3
INTRODUCTION	5
REINCARNATION	7
FIRST MEETING	14
UNCOMFORTABLE VISIT	16
THE NEXT MORNING	22
MEETING CONRAD	25
THE RESTAURANT	32
GOING BACK UNDER	42
WHO WAS CONRAD?	44
SAMMY THE KURD	49
SEEING NOAH	63
SAVED BY SHULON	65
FILLING IN DR. CINDY	76
PLEISTOCENE WRITINGS	82
RAHAB DESTRUCTION	85
IMPORTANT RETURN	88
OH NO!	90
VENUS DESTRUCTION	95
ATLANTIS	103
NOT A DEMON!	110
CONRAD'S RESCUE	114
INVISIBILITY	118
MYSTIFIERS	121
ESCAPE	123
WILL THERE BE DEATH?	126

BACK TO THE DEMON	128
COLLECTION	134
RETRIEVAL	137
THE FLOOD	143
JACK'S FIRE	148
NEW REVELATION	149
EARLY FLIGHT	157
RETRIBUTION	162
SCHOOL	168
SATURDAY	171
MEETING NOAH	173
CONRAD'S FAMILY	175
JOTHAN'S FAMILY	177
REECE'S FAMILY	179
BARTLET'S FAMILY	182
MARTIN'S FAMILY	184
FINDING LAND	187
TIME TO EAT AND YOGA	190
VISITORS	196
CAINITES	199
RESTAURANT	202
MONDAY	204
CALM BEFORE THE STORM	207
ATTACK	212
CONSIDERATIONS	216
ABOUT THE AUTHOR	225

Introduction

Hello reader! My name is James Manfred and my life is a mess. I guess you could say I've been given a gift, but using it will take some doing. My talent is that I can sense and control my soul. That seemingly little thing has caused some amazing things to happen to me; including a type of time travel or retrograded predestination; and a realistic understanding of what scientists call participatory Anthropics. Because of my gift, I have been sent back in time to fix wrinkles caused by our present reality and time being changed because of life. In our modern age we catch some of these glitches on camera. As shown in the following traffic camera footage from Australia May 9, 2012 at 3:33AM; a man on a bike disappears as a man appears; they both disappear and are seen on the edge of the road all within about a second so the man is not killed by "changing our normal reality".

Another traffic camera sees a similar event where a girl tries to cross the street and is snatched to the other side of the street within a second to save her life. This also changed our normal reality.

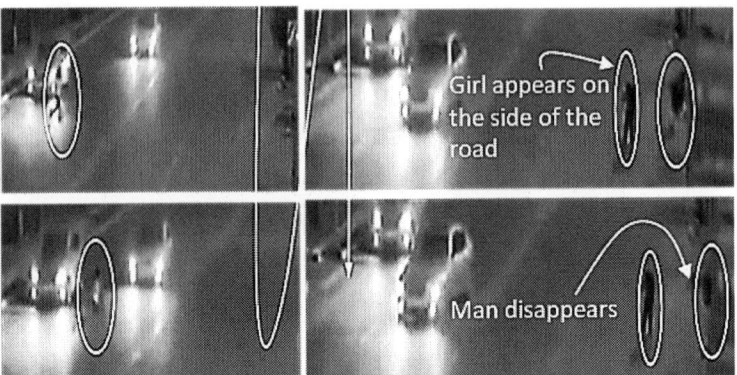

moving at superhuman speed, a man snatches a little girl just in time before she gets hit by a vehicle and then immediately disappears

These events don't affect our reality because scientists tell us our reality is continuously rewritten. They characterize this by saying the present is real and both the future and PAST are continuously modified to associate with the NEW present. Most changes don't affect the past drastically, but after hundreds and thousands of years, the past must change so events connect together. My job is to help with those changes. Because the past uses the same souls as we currently use, for the most part. There is always a link to the past. I must use this link when required to "fix" things.

To make this scientific oddness even more important; Einstein's Relativity model, and Neils Bohr's Quantum Physics describe reality as having no absolute time so the past and present can be co-resident but people cannot cross over. For physical bodies, one cannot jump from the present, because the speed of light limit must be violated. This is not an obstacle for our souls. All that is needed is to be aware of your soul and something called reincarnation. I have been given this awareness beyond the time most have it, but just about everyone has this awareness initially.

Reincarnation

Many children remember their past lives, but most of these memories fade by the time children are 10 years old. Therefore, there are so many researchers, today who have essentially proven this by questioning children, and researching their answers for accuracy. Sometimes, the children even remember, without learning it, a previous language they used in a previous life. Dr. Stevenson devoted well over forty years to the scientific documentation of past life memories of children from all over the world. He collected over 3000 cases. Arnall Bloxham, before him, studied 400 similar reincarnations with similar success. Anyone who wants to find out about these reincarnations can simply read one of the hundreds of books transcribing thousands of memories.[1] Let me give you a few examples.

- **John-the-Baptist**-6BC- Remembering he was Elijah, jumped for joy at least a month before he was reborn when he came near Jesus. Soon he would be called John-the-Baptist and eventually not remember anything about his previous life. This event was recorded in 10 Biblical books or more. ***Matthew 17:10-13-*** *'The scribes say that Elijah must come!' Jesus said, 'Elijah has come. The disciples understood that he had spoken of John the Baptist.[his reincarnation]*
- ***Mark 10:29-30-Jesus described reincarnation this way-***"*No one who has left brother or mother or children for me will*

---

[1] ***Researches in Reincarnation and Beyond*** in 1942 by AR Martin, Nicholas Spanos- multiple studies 1990s, and many, many more.

fail to receive a hundred times as much <u>in this present age</u> - brothers, mothers, and children...and <u>in the age to come</u>."

- **Bridey Murphy**- 1953-She remembered distinct details of her life as a 19th century Irish woman but the memories faded over time.
- **Shanti Devi**-1926-At 4 years old she remembered intimate details of her life as a woman named Ugdi Bai and her husband Pandit Kedarnath Chaube. Research showed everything she remembered had happened just like she remembered. Then the memories faded.
- **The Pollack twins**-1957- Both remembered intimate details of lives before they were 5. Then their memories began to fade.

On and on you could find out about reincarnation described in the Biblical accounts and in modern testimony. The reason I brought all that up was that I am slightly different in that I can relive those reincarnations even now. All I need is a little focus and the ability to temporarily free my soul.

This continuous soul through long time periods means that changes in reality put strain on this strange thread of life. Therefore the past must be, periodically changed to stay in SEQUENCE with our present reality. I know this sounds like a word puzzle, but it is how our universe is made.

My "normal job" is as a Biogenetic Anthropologist, history Professor, and ancient-dirt-digger which helps me get the "Focus" I told you about. Anyway! I have had some close calls and unbelievably blessed events happen to me as I help keep the past working.

I guess you could call me a Time-Fixer.

This series of books details something really strange that I, sort of, controlled; what I witnessed; the trouble I got into; and how

I, eventually, helped the past stay the past, first hand. I can't explain exactly how, but I will, explain what happened, who it happened to, how it affected the past and how it affected my life and the lives of those who help me. Forget that 2 of my helpers are demons and just learn about our crazy past and how time works.

While physicists are just now understanding how flexible this thing, we call reality, is; I lived and still live in an experiment that changes me, time after time. By some guiding hand, events are assured, to allow for our present understanding of our past and the past must be erased and rewritten over and over again. While I don't know what is next for me, this series of books describe what I know and have witnessed so far. As I said, the past and future both change to allow the "now" to stay real for cognitive observers [People with souls]. Here are some brief excerpts of what you will find in the first three adventures.

Time Fixer, the Beginning- This first book *details events I modified along with a courageous biologist my soul used to inhabit. My name or the old guy's name was Conrad; and he lived during the last part of the Pleistocene Age 10-thousand-years-ago. What a scary time! Luckily, I get an unusual "friend" along the way to ensure the known birth of the Holocene Age.*

Time Fixer, in India- The second book *details events I witnessed and modified along during my trip back to what history has called the Bharata War, 5-thousand years ago. This 'cleaning' required me to revisit Conrad to ensure the known development of an Indian Nation, Egyptian Nation, and a new type of human.*

Time Fixer, in Egypt- *The third book details events I witnessed and had to modify along with a Scythian Prince, Egyptian Kings, Amalekite Kings, an Ethiopian King, and a guy named Moses to save three nations.*

If you can't tell from the descriptions of the "books", let me say It out loud, *"I'm pretty messed up in my 'normal' life. I don't typically communicate well with others, which is weird because I am a University Professor. I don't date, I stay by myself, when I'm not teaching, and I almost always wear gloves so I don't touch anyone. While I do some writing, I always use an assumed name so that I can stay as invisible as I can. But like everything, changes are about to find me."*

I'd like to just tell you how everything happened, but, I'm not sure myself. What I do know is, somehow, I have linked with or traveled into the past and I came back---many times. I know some are thinking that's impossible and even if it could happen, some type of time rift would drastically change the present because of paradox. The truth is I smooth out paradox. If you kill your father before you were born would you exist? The answer is; somehow you would, but there would be someone like me who would be "sent" to move things around to ensure the past is secured.

I'm rambling a bit, but, somehow, I need you to understand that time must continuously be fixed to support our reality. It's like getting coffee grounds in your coffee. You really should remove the grounds so your coffee tastes better. Instead of cleaning coffee, I sort-of clean time itself and, like I said; there may be many "time-fixers" and all must have a good understanding about the time they are fixing.

Fixing the Pleistocene-To fix this first time-problem, I will be thrust way back to the Pleistocene Age. Many, calling themselves scientists, continue to ignore thousands of pieces of evidence concerning the civilized people who lived during the Pleistocene, so I'm certain, some may have difficulty about how my travels affected those outcomes. That's where a number of sacred ancient Jewish texts that were used by Moses to complete his "Genesis" book will help. One is called *"Generations of*

Adam" which describes many of the advanced kingdoms known in the Eastern Continent before the Pleistocene Extinction. I would get a chance to interact with those from the kingdoms of Shulon, Enoch, Palai, and Hanar and even see the great Anak people who lorded over many kingdoms. I know most of you have been isolated from the thousands of pieces of evidence about the highly-technological structure of the Pleistocene Age, so you I will provide tiny pieces of the evidence including historical records of the Babylonians, Assyrians, Egyptians, Indians, Chinese, Mongulala of Brazil, and so many more to help you understand as we go along and I describe what I saw.

This is one of the reasons I am an Archeologist as I studied dozens and dozens of the ancient histories to try to spot elements that needed to be worked on. I am concerned that, at some time, my job will force me to end my own past-life somehow, but so far, that has never come up.

Who Were the Anak?-Unfortunately, some of you have never heard of the Anak Giants. These people ruled the world for thousands of years. While the term Anak might seem strange, you may already know about them as they are also known as Nephilim, in Judeo-Christian histories. The Mongulala, in Brazil, called them the Akamim. In North America, they were called the Archaics. The Greek called them Olympians and the Dravidians of India called them the Arya. In Egypt, they were known as the Lords of Amenti, and the Sumerians called them Annunaki. Take your pick; these people ruled over all the lands before and even after the Pleistocene Extinction. Anak lived longer than the Cro-Magnon so they ruled large groups of individual kingdoms as if they were gods. I had to confront some of these guys and let me tell you they can be very scary.

What are Demons?-We are told in many Babylonian, Sumerian, Greek and many other histories including Judeo-Christian texts that when Anak people died, their souls were released, but unlike our souls, they were cursed so their souls did not enter a new body or go to sleep as ours do. Instead, they remain wandering outside of reality with no light, no comfort, no tasting, no sensations at all; only misery. Many call this group of unfortunates; demons. The only way for them to relieve their horror is to possess humans or animals. Let me tell you this one warning, NEVER let anyone tell you demons are not real. I have personal knowledge. In fact, I'm possessed right now. Sorry to spring that on you, but for me it has become a very important part of my job as some demons--- very few--- are trying to steer away from the evil that has been caused over time. I probably shouldn't have said anything yet, so just forget it until I explain later

Causes of Destruction-Besides just meeting these Anak characters, my mission was much more important in that I helped setup the conditions for some pretty important people to survive the almost complete destruction of the Earth. The earth didn't just one day decide to destroy itself at the end of the Pleistocene. It would take some time to cause the massive axis shift and I can tell you, dozens of texts from around the world, including 4 books of the Bible [*Psalms, Isaiah, Job, and Enoch*] and many more secular histories, described the destruction of the Planet Venus near the end of the Pleistocene, the destruction of one of the central commerce sites by flooding, and a massive shift in the Earth's axis all just before worldwide extinctions that ended the Pleistocene. Details of these events are echoed over and over again in ancient texts around the world and I was going to witness and 'clean' these events first hand--- without dying.

Artifacts-Hopefully, you are beginning to see a different image of the Pleistocene than the complete lie, established by those with blinders on. This lie has been pushed down the throats of our students in high Schools and colleges. The Pleistocene was not a time when Neanderthal came around grunting and pulling on a female's hair or even a place where the Flintstones lived.

Don't be confused by the limited metallic artifacts as metalworks have completely rusted away. We still have ancient stories written down on stone, bones, artwork, and even details of the clothes these people wore. In my "travels", I would find out the stories, images, and all the rest were more correct than anyone would think.

My Class and Anger Issues-In my classes I never hid the truths of the past because I knew what had happened through first-hand experience and why the events had to happen to make our present world exist. Sometimes, this got me in trouble and sometimes I was very lucky and was able to open the eyes of very impressionable students. OK! Sometimes I used my demon friend, but let me get started from the beginning so you can be helped as well. Please forget I said demon again. It's not what you think.

Right now let me apologize for all this front end stuff, but, so many have been misled by what I call Consensus-Quasi-Scientists who decided what they wanted to be true and have been trying to push "all the truth out of life" to support their consensus.

First Meeting

I suppose my story starts like many requiring a mixed-up memory that must be understood more clearly, as I was asked to see a psychologist for my, seemingly, deteriorating mood at work. After all, I was a professor of Anthropology and needed to project the image of the university and not alienate my students. Some thought I would get especially moody when we studied Pleistocene civilizations, but they had no idea of my past. I tried to fill my students with a closer approximation of truth, but there was always pressure to stay with the "required" text details. Even with the pressure, I would always add something to allow them to think beyond what some half-truth, consensus generated, "evolution-as-a-reality" Anthropological text. Up until a few years ago, it was easier to convince me concerning the normal descriptions of the development of mankind legitimacy, but all that changed.

Three and a half years ago, I was yanked out of my body into an ancient world for the first time.

I had been studying the remains of the worshipping sites called Gobekli Tepe, in southern Turkey, but my experience there went well beyond bizarre and it affected my whole life. As one of the oldest well-made structures to have remained intact for 12 thousand years; it had to be one of the major studies in my class, but my sensitivity about the area was no excuse for having a tantrum, they tell me.

One of my students, named Jake, had jumped up when I had explained about the extreme age, the wonders, the high level of technology, and precision workmanship of the Gobekli site in Turkey.

He puffed himself up and yelled out, *"Excuse me, but that is bull! People lived like animals back then. You seem to be trying to change history because some have timed the site wrong! You can't change history to suit some personal agenda."*

I don't know exactly what I told, the unappreciative, dimwitted, arrogant, young man, blinded by reconstructed, agenda driven historical details, but after throwing him out of my classroom, I really had to apologize and it got me a trip to a shrink. My opinion was that my student should have been thrown out for believing the garbage that others had been suggesting as anthropology. My boss, Dean of Historical Studies, had been "counseled" before he had me come to his office. I believe he was the closest person I had as a friend in the University, but this was a second time my students disrespected the ancient workings of the Pleistocene people which sort of got under my skin and there was not going to be a third.

"Go get someone to talk to you and you will be able to deal with those knuckle-heads much better", Dr. Sam Jenkins said. Sam was really a good guy and besides being a Doctor of History, I really liked him. I promised I would--he came back with a "REALLY?" --and I again told him I was going.

Just to be sure he had already made an appointment and had someone assigned as a substitute for my class when I was supposed to go. Did I tell you he had already been counseled?

Uncomfortable Visit

I went to the address on the piece of paper Sam gave me. The building was old and paint was peeling on the window sills. I was thinking I knew what type of psychologist he would be. He probably looked like he had paint-chips coming off his wrinkled skin and so old he would use a cane. As I entered the psychologist's office I saw a great looking woman with a name that started with "Doctor". *"Oh! Boy! This was worse than I thought"*, I said to myself, so I took off one of my gloves and shook her hand; then I went over and sat in a chair. Yes, I have that "Dr", as part of my name but my degree was not in flim-flam. I'm sorry I didn't tell you about my gloves before but I know you were already confused.

This woman was using her "womanly charms" to advance herself as a real doctor. She wore a nice looking, flowery, dress and shoes with a little bit of a heel. While the dress wasn't really short, she did have long legs that I could not help noticing. Her face was a pretty nice one and her hair was long and well brushed, but I was not going to let any of that affect me. I would need to talk to her and get some *"You love your mother"* answer that I could tell SAM. Then, I could go back and do what made me feel important while keeping my rage under control.

Dr. C.L. Martin said *"Hello! How are you?"*, and I said, *"Fine."* Then, I looked at my shoes to not give her too much recognition.

She began again, *"My name is Cindy, what is yours?"* I sort of grunted back, *"My name is James; James Manfred. My friends call be J-Man."* I didn't tell her I really didn't have many live friends.

She took out a notebook and sat across from me and asked, *"What is the problem Mr. J-man?"* As she said this, she made her face show her dimples to try to make me want to be there or some other foolish thing, but I just ignored her all the more.

I came back with *"I've had a lot on my mind lately and I guess I have been pushing people away, including my students. It was strongly suggested that I have someone talk to me about it."* I tried to sound more professor-like so she could understand I was going to be in charge of this process.

She went on and said. *"When you feel like it, just tell me why you think you might be feeling this way and we'll find a way to make you feel better."* She smiled and asked if I needed water, a pillow, or a cookie.

"Who puts cookies out for patients?" I couldn't help myself as my hand picked up one of the cookies and my mouth did the rest. To make it worse, the cookies were really good! For some reason, this Doctor Cindy had already made me feel at ease. My pretense just vanished and I began telling her my problems like a gushing fire hose. Maybe it was something in the cookie I had tasted. —I took another.

"I guess it's been building for a long time, but I have recently let my moodiness affect me more. I don't go out with others and I don't really attempt conversations beyond what is needed to accomplish my job. My research, typically, fills my days while reading and TV fill my evenings when I am not out in some archeological dig trying to find out more about man's past." I briefly looked up to see if she was impressed with my exotic travels, but she just wrote more notes."

I tried to stop myself from telling my darkest secrets, but something inside me kept pushing me.

"Maybe, I had better start some time ago. When I was 15 years old, something freeky happened. I had been deathly sick for

almost 2 weeks. I didn't even tell my dad I was sick as he was always preoccupied and my mom had passed away a couple years earlier. I just took cold showers to get my temperature below 103^0, stayed covered as much as possible, downed vitamin Cs, and felt sorry for myself. Finally, I seemed to be getting over whatever it was, so I went to the local zoo with someone I thought was a friend. His name was Jimmy---"Jimmy-the-blabber" should have been his name.".

I looked up to see if she was listening, all I saw was that she was taking all types of notes. Possibly, it was a shopping list or doodles of unicorns and such, but I decided to go on, just the same.

"I love the zoo animals and was at this "gorilla encounter" thing. As I stretched over the protection wall, I noticed a fairly large bunch of coarse hair that looked like it was from the gorilla. I was mesmerized by the power of this gorilla named "Mombo", he was pounding his chest and jumping up and down to show another gorilla, named "Gentry", he was boss and was going to eat first. This is when things got weird. When my hand touched the hair, I could, somehow feel the intensity of the anger of this gorilla".

I looked up to try to get my composure and see if she was giggling or anything, but she was still writing and I continued, *"Let me explain what I mean. I seemed to be part of him, just by touching his hair."* I took a sip of water and continued.

"I had heard about people called sensitives or empaths on TV, in Phycology, and in science fiction books, and the feelings I had, seemed somewhat like I believed those people would feel, but more intense. The whole ideal seemed too fictiony for me, but I was still feeling strange.

I looked up again and added, *"I could feel the gorilla's strength when he pounded his hand on a log, then I felt his breathing and his desire to be in control. I felt his contempt for his captors. As I jerked my hand away from the hair, my "vision" simply left and things were spinning. My friend told me; I fainted for a little while. When I came back to my senses, my "buddy" was looking at me and had even called 911. My embarrassment would continue as those in school were "advised" of my weakness and called me "the fainter" for quite some time. I hated what happened, but now I realize, it was the beginning of my search for man's true history. This could be a good thing, but it has made me, sort of, stand-offish. ----- I'll never be like others."*

During High School, a similar incident happened when this guy had gotten mad at me for tripping and almost pushing him to the ground. To steady himself and show he was going to pound me, he grabbed my arm. As I apologized, I could "feel" his anger leaving, as if I "caused" his anger to reduce. I thought I was going to eat dirt and he simply went away. I also, somehow, knew his dad had beat him the night before.

Cindy looked up from her writing and tried to comfort me by saying, *"I think everyone feels like that quite often. You may be blowing things out of proportion and feel threatened by communication with those around you. Your father, maybe, didn't have time for you and possibly you had a difficulty making new friends. We are going to try some mental exercises to relieve your insecurities and disappointments together. It will be fun, you will feel so much better, and I know you will love it."* She seemed truly concerned, but initially, I thought she was being condescending and thought I was making up the whole thing after reading a SiFi book or something.

I just smiled and said, *"Here is what I know. Your favorite color is purple, which I think is just wrong and your middle name is Lynne, which you hate. You have a Scottish terrier named Ben that is the love of your life, currently. You are not dating anyone right now, but almost a year ago you broke up with a guy named*

Mike who had one ear larger than the other and he smelled of Garlic any time he would eat anything that had the slightest amount of the stuff in it. You love westerns, rock music, and Chinese food. You had half of a peanut butter sandwich before coming to work and are trying to decide if you should paint your living room light green or tan." I could tell she was extremely shocked and felt violated.

"Why did I say all that stuff?" I yelled to myself. I hit myself on the head and looked down at the floor as if I could remove myself from the awful feeling I had just induced.

She stayed silent for a while. Like me, she wouldn't even look at me, but she was trying to hold back her anger. Her top lip even was shaking. She was even clicking her pen in and out.

I don't even know why I had just done that and I felt terrible. Here I was, this great time traveler, and I could not go back 20 seconds to stop my stupid mouth. I apologized after seeing her so distraught and saw, not only the outward anger and disgust, but I could feel her empty, sadness inside. I apologized again and then a third time. I told her I would not do that anymore, but I thought she needed to know I had a real problem not a social ineptitude. OK! She was right about that, but that was not causing my recent bouts with anger.

At my pathetic apology, she laughed a little; then she wiped away a tear from one eye and said, *"I guess you do have --- something. Sorry I acted poorly. I'm supposed to be helping you. Please don't do whatever you did anymore and I promise to make sure you know I am truly trying to help!" Let's start over. Hello, my name is Cindy and I dated a guy with garlic breathe who are you?"*

I said, "Hello, *I'm James*." I, then told her I was sorry again and that I would not invade her privacy anymore. I explained, that when I focus and come in close contact with cells or DNA, I can feel things, like what happened with the stupid angry guy. I showed her I had my gloves on. To make it up to her, I told her stuff about me. *"I like my name and my favorite color was brown like your eyes, I mean like dirt. No! I'm not saying your eyes look like dirt, but I'm trying tell you stuff about me that is just as personal. I, also, used to have a dog, named Cranky, but he passed away.* I told her, *"I also liked westerns, Chinese food, and rock music and I had never dated someone with 2 different ear sizes."* Then I added, *"My home is in bad need of painting so I'm not sure what color it is. I think it is an off-white-----way-off."*

Dr. Cindy looked like she was getting over being freaked out and said, *"I'm glad you don't think my eyes look like dirt and I'm sorry about being Cranky."*

I said, *"No! my dog's name is Cranky, you are just fine."*

She was getting me mixed up but then she said, *"Let's continue tomorrow. I'm certain just telling someone about all this will help some and we'll figure out something for the rest. I promise."* So, I agreed and began to leave. Dr. Cindy grabbed me by the hand as I got up and she told me almost in a whisper. *I know I will be able to help you even if I don't know exactly what you are going through. Please trust me.* All I was thinking was she doesn't know the half of it and I wondered if it was a bad thing to tell her things I knew she would not understand. As I left I said, *"I'll be back!"*

The Next Morning

We had agreed to meet the next day in the morning and I was there at 8AM. Dr. Cindy was already set up and, sure enough, cookies were on the table.

Cindy decided she would try to recap what she thought she understood and she seemed to have understood more than I thought. I believed the whole soul making contact with others and me being cognizant of my soul's actions would have been considered fantasy, but she was matter of fact about everything. Maybe she was just playing me to get me to come back. Maybe she thought I was a nut-job and just trying to establish the level of Schizophrenia. This next session should give me the insight I needed as I concurred with her notes about me and I began a second time.

"While I usually stayed by myself, I had a girlfriend in 11th grade. Her name was Sharon and she was in my earth science class. I wasn't long before I ruined that relationship. Not from anything she did. She was great and I liked her a lot, but I touched her and something went horribly wrong as I looked and where she had been I was looking at a coal-miner who had a strange look on his face. He was dirty and smoking and rough and crude---somehow my girlfriend was a guy. I didn't understand the whole past life thing and it freaked me out. I jumped back and I don't even remember what I said, but I do know every time I saw her I could help thinking about that man-inside her. I decided aloneness was something I had to endure.

Cindy was writing faster than ever and finally stopped me and asked if she could record our session and listen to it a second time when she wrote her notes later so she would not miss some of the complexity she was witnessing. I agreed she started a tape and I continued.

In College, I was lucky enough to get to a dig in Cairo, Egypt at the site of a lesser king of Egypt named Khendjer. I had contacted Dr. Merser during the year and told him of my interest in Archeology. He would be thankful I helped him as I was digging and loving it when I came to a piece of text with a Hebrew word for King and the Egyptian word for "Ra or On" When I showed him what I found he could not contain himself. He had been collecting evidence about a Hebrew king of Egypt during the 13th Dynasty who ruled near where the ruins of Khendjer's Pyramid complex was in Saqqara and whose wife was the daughter of the High Priest of On. His Biblical name was Joseph and her name was Queen Asenath *his Pyramid was about 140 meters high and her pyramid was about 60 meters high. Khendjer ruled with Amenemhet VI and the pyramids at that time were made out of baked bricks covered with limestone facing. Once the facing was gone, the pyramids all but disappeared except for the underground causeways and tombs.* I showed Cindy images of Khendjer that we found and a reconstruction of his pyramid complex.

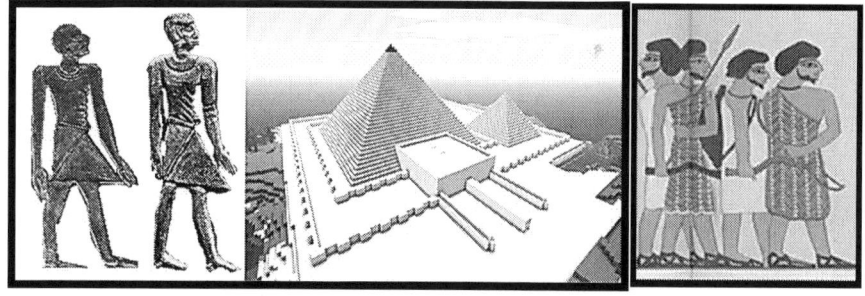

Dr. Merser would go on writing a paper about the finding of Joseph's pyramid, and he even mentioned me in it. What he didn't know was something very strange. As I found the piece of inscribed stone, I felt "myself" as a wealthy Jewish man, inside the pyramid, examining the workmanship. I was dressed in a fancy tunic similar to those described on temple walls [See the Drawing above] and I was admiring my friend's new gold inlayed sandals. It all happened in a second, but I could even smell the mustiness of the pyramid I would find held the body of Joseph. I had sort-of gone back in time to about 1730BC.

The next 2 summers I was able to go with Dr. Merser on other digs. I knew I wanted to be an Archeologist and that I could experience something about the past more than just seeing rocks.

There were a few weird flashes and confirmations I understood from these random images, but it would me much more pronounced, after I had graduated and become an adjust professor. Today, I am a professor and freelance Biological Anthropologist known for being able to date artifacts accurately and understand who did what. These insights were from my dissociative soul I've been talking about. As an anthropologist, I write papers for various journals, mostly under an assumed name, and I conduct research for Jasmine-Carter University where I teach. This is done by submitting a research description and receiving grants by various alumni and from the University itself, if the right people think discovery could add acclaim to the University. I had written a number of articles about mankind during the Pleistocene, especially around the Sumerian area and Gobekli Tepe and that got me over to Turkey. The trip got me involved with a man I called Conrad, but I'm getting ahead of myself. I think the best thing here is to start from my first study trip to Turkey a few years ago."

She said, *"This is great, but I want you to focus on details so we can see if you can reduce your demons."* I laughed out loud when she said "demons". She had no idea how associated with that word, my story would be.

Meeting Conrad

"Anthropological studies usually had me digging in the dirt in out of the way places around the world. From bones, pieces of pottery, structures, and various dating methods, I try to determine what happened in an area. While digging in the 12 thousand-year-old, 20-building complex now known as Gobekli Tepe [The stupid name is Turkish for Potbelly Hill], <u>I came across what looked like a purse made out of stone.</u> While these things have been found all over the world, the only representation of three purses in Gobekli was an image on one of the upright stanchions that had supported one of the larger temples."

I stopped my story and went out to my car for my computer. Then I pulled up a site that had a number of the stone purses that have been found around the world before I continued. I pointed out to her that the one I found was similar to the 4th one on the top row.

Cindy, I mean Dr. Cindy said, *"These things are the stupidest things I've ever seen. Why would anyone carry one of these things around?"* I reminded her of belly-bags, back-packs, telephones the size of suitcases, the old boom-boxes, monster sized pierced earrings, and nipple chains worn by bikers.

She said, *"You made your point---Continue."*

I also showed her a picture of the dig site and pointed to the location of the purse find on the left of the image, but she didn't seem to see any more than dirt and old stanchions.

I told her, *"While I was rubbing the purse to see if any writing of significance was on it, something amazing happened "again". Just like my earlier encounters, but much more real. I surmised, I came in contact with viable DNA on the strange stone and this time, things got really weird. It violated everything I knew about time and even after having little glimpses of the past before, I truly was terrified. I could feel what I felt with the boy I almost had to fight in my own times. I did not believe my insight this time had been modern. It frightened me a little after all this time and everything I had gone through. How stupid is that?"*

Cindy said, *"Calm down and breathe. Do you need a break?"*

After drinking a glass of water and taking another one of Cindy's homemade cookie creations, I continued. *"I "felt" like I had "joined" another person. Not a person from today, this was a person associated with the "stone purse" I had excavated. I was "in the head" of this man. It was like I became him, but wasn't him. It seemed something like what I believe demons do when they possess people, but I was not trying to do something nefarious, in fact, I didn't even know, really, how I got there."*

Dr. Cindy was not just recording, she was writing as fast as I was talking. I assumed she was writing nutcase, straight jacket, shock therapy, and lobotomy, but I continued anyway. I thought, *"If she asks me how to spell lobotomy, I'm out of here."*

She didn't, so I continued, *"Later, I would find out the name of the man that I had "invaded" was Conrad, or at least that is what I "felt" his name was, but right now I was in shock. I could see what he was seeing and was feeling his will or his being. I don't know how to explain it exactly, but there I was, possibly 12 thousand years ago, experiencing life, inside another person. Conrad began to speak to someone and I could "feel" what he was saying. Unfortunately, this was too much of a shock and just like what happened years before, I blacked out again. Waking up after fainting, my helper, "Sammie" indicated he had been watching over me."*

I stopped for a breather and told the "Doctor" that my friend and guide's name was really Samo-cara-thaa-ban-in, but he allowed my Americanization. Together, we went to his home town in Urfa about 7-miles from the dig site. Luckily, I had brought several items with me to help describe my story to this woman who was examining my insanity. On the computer, I showed her where Ulfa and the dig site were in the southern area of Turkey in the middle of the Muslim group known as Kurds. Then I continued.

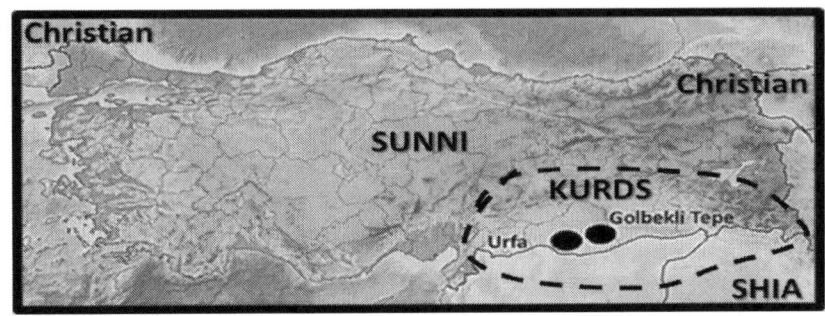

"Sammie suggested I stay at his home that night as he was still worried about me. Sammy was one of the Kurdish people of this beautiful land and had become a great friend during the dig. In the morning, I was thinking about what had happened and like I explained earlier; how quantum physics and participatory Anthropics had indicated time, space, matter, and energy were all built from the same characteristic and based on perception of a cognizant viewer. I was explaining to myself, this is why Schrodinger's cat was able to be both dead and alive at the same time until grounded by cognition."

I quickly looked up and luckily my doctor must have seen "Big Bang" on the television and already heard about the seemingly impossible reality of Schrödinger's cat, so I continued, *"The science community calls this combining force of everything, including time and space, "Quantum fluctuations". By increasing or decreasing the fluctuations, time could be instantly converted to space, or energy. For some reason, I remembered gold fluctuated at about 600 exahertz [10^{18} hertz] and slowing it down to 400 exahertz converted "it" to Hydrogen. I surmised that my "soul" could change the vibrational pattern depending on an outward sensation like the "vibrational pattern of a similar DNA". Like everything else, DNA fluctuations were used to interact with reality. In our bodies, DNA signal nearby cells to repair wounds or replicate and testing has shown these fluctuations are in near visible light spectrums about 1 petahertz*

[10^{15} hertz]. Just as a guess, the DNA fluctuations of two similar beings could possibly build "beat frequencies" associated with time to convert or change it." My soul had not constraints of time as it associated with a DNA Structure and fed off the reality established around it.

Cindy stopped me and made that stupid sign where you flatten you hand and pass it over your head. Then she told me she didn't understand a word and; what were exahertz and a petahertz----- and what is a cognizant observer?

I apologized and explained, *"Exahertz and Petahertz were just very fast vibrations no one could hear or sense with your eyes; then I explained that a cognizant-observer is a viewer of reality that has a soul. You could say, our souls actually hold reality "together" for the viewer and when no souls are around, there is no reality."* I told her, *"Only people have these souls so a dog or a tree cannot affect reality; only us."* I pointed to her and then to me and then explained that I was simply trying to understand in my own head how time could possibly be changed by touching the stone purse. She was already trying to figure out how to spell Petahertz before I added the part that would really get her confused.

I was certainly learning more about this soul we have in and around us, but I knew enough to not dwell on this very important part of living right now or Dr. Cindy's brain might explode. To get rid of all the technical stuff, I asked her if she had ever heard of the "power of positive thinking" or "Self Actualism". Unbelievably, she had read about Maslow's "Self Actualism" discovery a few months before meeting me as it is sort of a Psychology thing.

I indicated, *"My understanding is, <u>self-actualism</u> happens because your soul extend itself and allow intimate change in reality."*

I then told her. *"It seems that, somehow, "my soul" can be sent into the past, because no-one's soul is specifically tied to this reality. This travelling is heightened if the entity I am linked with is a body that my soul had been part of in the past."*

You guessed it; that hit the limit of understanding for her so I backed away. There is a lot to learn about what reality is; our soul-what it does and how it does it; and the concept we have about time. For me it was more important to understand simply because I was doing things that were impossible and in the center of it all was my "soul". My soul was me or could communicate with me or it surrounded me or all of the above. Now I, or that part of me, could travel back in time and connect with another person who had died thousands of years before I was born.

Only later would I understand that this Conrad guy was me in an earlier life. I had somehow stumbled on DNA of myself and my Soul was reactivated as Conrad.

Cindy became excited. *"How could I been a Psychologist all of these years, have studied works of those called great Psychologist and never have even comprehended this AT ALL!"* she yelled. She was almost mad at herself and truly intrigued. *"Help me understand."* She continued.

I went to my trusty laptop to show her a short paper on the "Soul controlling" and the new work that was going on to understand this important part of our being and how it allows us to leave the confines of our "reality". I could tell this was all new for her and this relatively new science was still not commonly known by everyone even with over 500 verses in our Bible specifically explaining over and over again how our heart [cognizant portion of our soul] has its own brain and how it controls communication between our self, our soul, and our spirit [triune existence]. I explained that somehow I was able to "release my soul" sort of like "astral projection" that you hear about except when "my DNA" came in contact with a foreign DNA, they, somehow, communicated or combined, or resonated, or something. If there was a soul connection, this connection didn't care about any <u>time difference</u>. Reincarnation was the key to time-travel.

I further explained that DNA to DNA communication happens millions of times a day. *"Our DNA communicates to nearby cells-all the time. The communication, convinces cells to begin healing after a cut or infection; or a CELL is told to change its characteristics; or DNA communication signals the generation and release of white blood cell armies. Scientists tell us most of the communication is done by the <u>vibrational variations allowed by the DNA Helix design</u>. It seems my DNA can talk more easily to nearby DNA and my soul can connect with a previous life."*

Dr. Martin put her pencil down and shook her head. Then she lifted her glasses and rubbed her eyes. Then she said, *"Well, Mr. super-Soul, I'm way too confused. Why don't we take a break and go get some Chinese food?"*

I was in shock. If I had only known that talking about bio-physics was the way to a woman's heart, I would not have spent so many lonely days. Trying not to sound needy, I said, *"Sure, I know just the place."* She got her coat and we left--- in separate cars.

The Restaurant

By the time we got to the restaurant, the time was way past the end of my appointment, so I thought I should leave out the scary details and simply have a nice meal with a friendly, good-looking, and, fun to be around, woman. Instead, the only thing she could talk about was how, what, when, where, and everything in between, so I continued. She said, *"Don't leave out a thing."* Strangely, she didn't have her notepad, but I brought my computer to show her examples that might help her understand.

To try to put some sense into what happened to me I began explaining in a little different way, *"While DNA can certainly disintegrate over extreme ages, there is no significant difference between live-DNA and what is called "dead-DNA", in fact, scientists are trying to bring Pleistocene Mammoth DNA back to life so they can make "New" mammoths and new soft tissue finds of Pleistocene dinosaurs like T-Rex now had scientists thinking about even more animals. Maybe, and I'm just guessing here; but here is what I believe. My empathic oddity allowed me to separate my soul and connect to a different timeline because reincarnated souls are never die."*

With that DNA stuff out of the way, I was thinking about continuing my description. Unbelievable, I had discuss technical things again, but she wasn't even yawning like every other woman with which I had previously "discussed" things. I took a few bites of food, that was not very hot now and, being nervous, I continued.

"I knew I needed to quit trying to determine what was happening and just let it happen as I had a burning desire to get back to the Pleistocene people for some reason I did not completely understand. I told my friend "Sammy" the details of my time travel experience and opened the sack holding the stone artifact. Just picking it up was enough. It wasn't long before my "soul" had again made a transition and I began experiencing my new surroundings. This Conrad guy had already been up for a while and had gone to work. You would never have believed this, but Conrad was a biologist of sorts. Possibly, that was part of the reason I could "link" with him as our training or mind-set was somewhat similar. I had seen a number of the artifacts and read a number of the ancient texts showing the high level of technology of the Pleistocene civilizations, but I was still shocked to see microscopes and particle separators that were somewhat familiar and even more advanced. On the lab workstations, dishes of fluids were being radiated with different colors and at differing rates and intensities. Artificial lighting and electricity were obviously in use and the laboratory was amazing. I wondered why we could not find evidence of this lab environment a mere 10 thousand years in the future but realized Iron would have completely disintegrated within 4 thousand years, buildings crumble and details of experiments would have vanished thousands of years ago and I also know everything in front of me would be swept away by a massive worldwide flood that would end the Pleistocene. I was seeing ancient art and science right before my eyes."

I explained to Cindy, I mean Dr. Cindy that a number of researchers had put forth the idea that highly advance aliens from another galaxy came to Earth and seeded us. They suggested that these visitors were the reason we keep finding evidence of a highly civilized race of humans that lived during the Pleistocene. I was finding, first hand, the civilized people were not alien, they were normal Cro-Magnon humans reaping the rewards of thousands of years of civilization and having lifetimes ten times as long as we have today and longer. Is an anthropologists, I knew there was no question that civilizations, lost the memories of this wonderful past and had to start over after the Bharata War 5500 years ago just like dozens of the ancient texts and all types of physical evidence told us. Right now, I was seeing people smarter than we are today, with slightly larger brains, and technology that had been around for a long time.

Dr. Cindy, looked up, twirled more noodles and said, *"This is great information, but you are going too fast. Remember, I study feelings not Anthropology and Biology. My brain is swimming."*

Backup Data

I had to slow down for the Doctor, so I'm wondering about you guys reading this detail of my life. Wherever I can, I will show you what I showed doctor so we can all connect. I'm placing the images in this book as we go along. I was pretty sure I needed her to understand how advance these people were or she would not be able to understand what I was going through but I didn't want her to fall asleep so I took a few bites of my quickly-getting-cold food and decided to show her what I meant with a few examples of Pleistocene technology and culture that had somehow weathered the millennia. Here is what I showed her.

The following collage shows a tiny portion of the intricate stone bases of massive machines found in South America alone. Nobody knows what the machines were and the wooden and metal parts are completely gone. But the complete elimination of the metal components suggests these were Pleistocene machines.

Next, I showed her some of the many examples of stone flooring made of materials that were "grown into shape" leaving no space between adjacent, odd shaped, manufactured stones from West Virginia, Oklahoma, and Australia. I let her know that this rock growing is evident around the world.

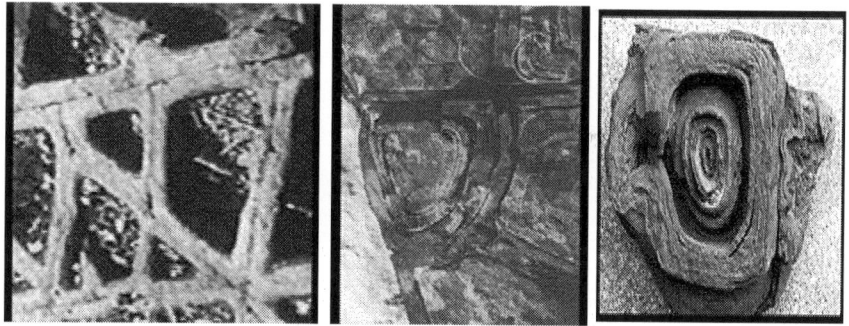

Then I showed her a couple of examples of petrified shoe prints. The first below, shows where the man crushed trilobites as he walked and the second image still shows the fine details of the shoe stitching. Trilobites became extinct a long time ago.

 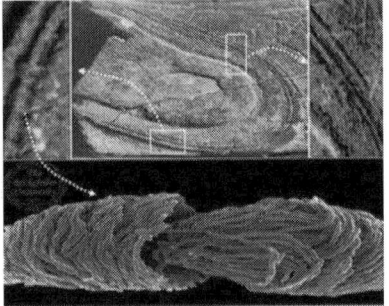

Next, I showed her the intricate artworks from Eurasia and carpentry hammer with a petrified wood handle and iron head. This, along with nails, and screws were found in the Americas from the Pleistocene.

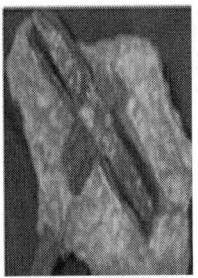  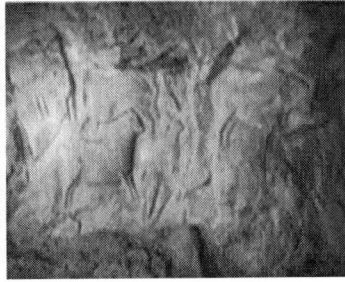

Finally, I showed her some of the many artifacts associated with ancient use of electricity including a battery now locked inside a geode and a small cash of batteries housed in clay containers from Iraq. The second row showed how ancient texts described a method to connect many batteries together for electroplating and various worked metals from extremely ancient times. To the right was an etching from early Sumeria, showing how their predecessors made AC electricity that would not be rediscovered until the early 20th century. The man at the top of the image is working cords back and forth to run the generator and electrify a globe into making sparks similar to some of Tesla's devices; and this was done way before Tesla was born.

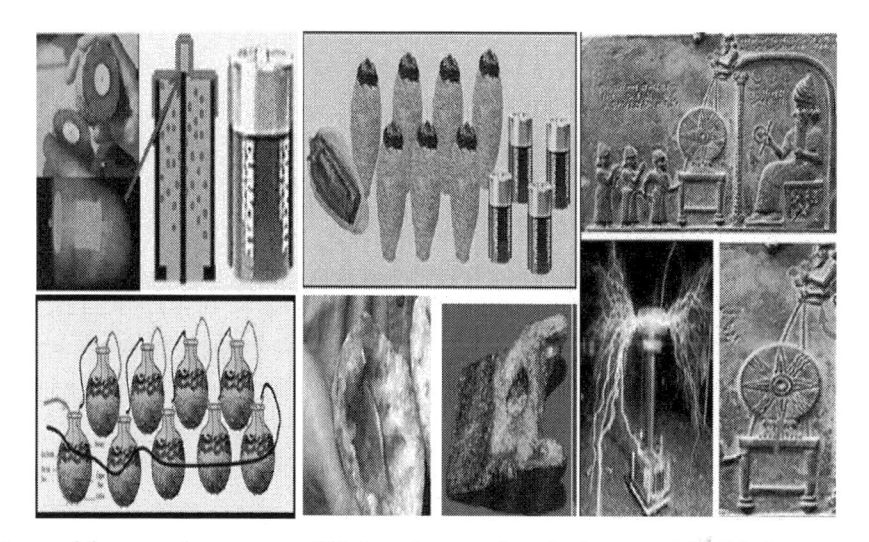

I could see she was still having a hard time with Pleistocene people being technologically advanced so I stopped for a minute to tell her about what modern biologists and researchers are finding. I showed her some of the hundreds of pieces of evidence of reconstructed dinosaurs, which were revitalized in the Pleistocene. Many were being found with <u>unfossilized soft tissues</u> making up T-Rex, Duckbills, and many other previously "extinct" animals. I explained fossilization typically occurs over a 50-thousand-year period, so the unfossilized dinosaurs were running around towards the end of the Pleistocene. I told her how, some of these unfossilized samples, including Mammoths and dinosaurs, have been found with "<u>viable DNA</u>" so it is known they were less than 20 thousand years old to account for the cell flexibility. Then I showed her the next images of unfossilized blood and connective tissues of a Tyrannosaurus Rex that must have been reconstructed by these Pleistocene Biologists. The graphic to the right shows some of the reconstructed previously Mesozoic-Age-animals. In a later journey I would even get to pet one of these creatures.

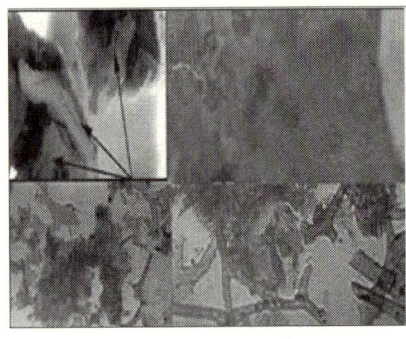

Somehow, Cindy had almost finished her meal, so I quickly ate about have of my General Tso chicken and I asked her if she would like desert and coffee. We ordered and the coffee got her excited again.

"Please go on James", she said, and quickly added, *"Can I call you James instead of J-Man?"* I laughed and said, *"You can call me anything you like. You have no idea, just talking about this seems to be helping this pent-up anger and fear I carry around."* She said, *"It's helping me as well. Now, I have stuff I can say to my book club friends when we get together. Not your life stuff; I mean all the ancient dinosaur making and reincarnation stuff."* I laughed, took a bite of this unusual desert and began to let her in on a strange new world I had seen.

Back To My Observations

In this ancient lab, I was actually seeing the remanufacture and modification of DNA and animals and my "host" was part of it. It was just like the Bible tells us that during this time most of the animals were "Abominations or Unclean".

Dr. Cindy, was shaking her head in confusion as many times, these facts are suppressed to assure a stronger grip of dogmatic views or consensus-controlled theories like undirected evolution. Anyway, I just wanted to give her details to help open her mind and I got back to my story and showed her a couple of the hundreds of text describing ancient biological manipulation.

Generations of Adam*[2] *6:1-5- *Among Adam's little ones was Ammah. Ammah <u>understood the secrets of creation</u>. She manipulated the very fountain of life until she had <u>created new forms of beings</u>. [8:4] Tranter learned the ways of his mother Ammah and <u>he did manipulate the very nature of man and beast to create new forms</u> which God had not ordained.*

Essene Bibles- Jasher 4:18-19- *and the sons of men in those days [Before the Flood] took <u>from the cattle</u> of the Earth,<u> the beasts</u> of the field and the <u>fowls</u> of the air, and taught the <u>mixture of animals of one species with the other</u>,*[3]

Then I continued. "Conrad went past a shiny surface and I got my first glimpse of my old me. He was tall and modern looking and he wore something that made me laugh; a medium length jacket and trousers extending slightly below the knees. It was just like the "business attire" found on giant skeletons in cavern homes under Death Valley as described in a 1947 copy of the Newspaper, *"Hot Citizen"*. Again, I showed her what I was talking about from a reprint in my laptop. I used to think it was a puffed-up observation, but maybe he really did see details from the time of Conrad.

Hot Citizen [1947]- According to Dr. Daniel Bovee and spokesman Howard E. Hill; *"The caves (below Death Valley) contained the skeletons of several gigantic men, each in the region of around <u>nine feet in height</u>. The caves contain mummies of men and animals and implements -<u>more advanced than ours</u>. A long tunnel*

---

2 **Generations of Adam-** *referenced in Genesis 5 and part of the Messianic-Essene Bible, Ethiopian Bible*
3 **Jasher-** *referenced in Joshua 10 and 2 Samuel 1, and part of the Messianic-Essene Syriac, and Ethiopian Bibles.*

> *from this ritual temple hall took the party into a room where, <u>well-preserved remains of dinosaurs</u>, saber-toothed tigers, imperial elephants and other extinct beasts were paired off in niches as if on display.*
> *"<u>These giants are clothed in garments consisting of a medium length jacket and trousers extending slightly below the knees. The texture of the material is said to resemble gray dyed sheepskin,</u> but obviously it was taken from an animal unknown today."*

She laughed and said, *"I think that style is coming back."* It seems fashion was the same around the world during the Pleistocene, but I needed to describe to her what I saw and felt so I would have someone to confide in as I went back to my story. Just telling someone this had lifted a huge weight off me.

"Somehow, my internal giggle had been noticed by Conrad who had no idea what was going on. He had laughed right in the middle of an experiment that appeared to be an attempt to modify the heart from the region of his DNA allele conversion. Startled, he just sat there confused. It was then I realized I might somehow be able to communicate with this guy 12-thousand years in the past."

My startled doctor simply said *"NO WAY!"*

"Yes way!" I continued; *"I tried concentrating on wiggling my fingers and unbelievably, Conrad was moving his fingers. He grabbed his hand quickly and left the lab. He went to the comfort area and shook his hand to halt the annoyance. I concentrated on blinking my eyes and this really got him as he started doing what I concentrated on. I decided I had better stay more passive so that I would not harm this ancient man anymore and as I thought about other things I found myself back in Gobekli with Sammy. I didn't pass out or anything. I quickly*

wrote down the details of my experience and told Sammy what was happening. We were both excited. OK; I was much more excited and I was ready to try some experiments to establish communication."

Going Back Under

Again, I touched the stone purse all over until I, again, was attached to Conrad. I was able to make him tap the table he was sitting at once. After waiting a short time, he, uncontrollably, tapped on the table twice, then 3 times, and then 4 times. I had his undivided attention and he yelled out. *"Who is there?"* With all my will I thought *"friend"* and he expressed something that I interpreted it as *"Friend?"* This was followed by *"from"* and *"future"* as I pushed out these impressions, or thoughts, or whatever they were. *"Yes, it sounded stupid, but I simply didn't know what to do,"* I told Dr. Cindy.

"Conrad was jumping around, looking behind himself, and almost crying. From nowhere he said to himself, *"Calm down!"*, but I was behind his compulsion.

"What do you want?", he cried out and he said to himself *"no harm"*. This seemed to be little concession for his building terror.

"How are you in my head?", he questioned, and he said back to himself, *"Soul Transfer"*.

While this doesn't seem like much I was completely drained just presenting this little communication and he said to himself, *"With you soon."*

I didn't leave right away. Instead, I just watched what he did, felt what he felt, and saw what he saw. Once I did the radio silence thing, Conrad was still talking to himself, but I stayed quiet so I could see what these people were like.

After a while, Conrad, got a drink of water, and went back to his lab and I could tell exactly what he was doing. He was DNA sequencing to make a map of the nucleotide sequence along a DNA string. The method he used we call Electrophoresis, where DNA samples are placed in a gel and exposed to an electric field to test electronegativity and character. Then he remotely added a string and did some type of process I was not understanding. The first and second strings combined, except a few areas where nucleotide differences would not allow combination. By sending the sample through 2 additional processes, the mismatch areas were gone and what I believe was a new DNA string had been born, which may have been the beginning of a new species or modified characteristic to make an animal stronger, or faster, or tastier.

I looked, I mean Conrad looked, down the lab and there must have been at least 20 biological designers in the same lab. They were building what Moses referred to as "UNCLEAN, abominable animals. Conrad looked like he was going to take a break and so did I as I released my concentration and I again was in the Desert of modern Turkey."

Who Was Conrad?

Once I got back to my own time, I started looking for all the potential people Conrad could be. Certainly, he could be one of the pure Cro-Magnon people, one of the Anak humans celebrated as giant gods, or one of the hybrid humans known as Gentiles in the Biblical history, or even one of the Neanderthal humans. All of these people were known to live before the end of the Pleistocene Extinction. The more information I had about this guy, the better will be my chances of successfully seeing the past which was, now, my new focused objective. Here is what I knew so far.

1. *He was fairly tall, but not gigantic.*
2. *He had light skin and possible a little reddish or had reddish hair and he looked like the reconstructed images of Cro-Magnon or some hybrid of that race.*
3. *He, apparently, lived in the Gobekli area and carried a stupid stone purse.*
4. *I felt like I was supposed to be there.*

I think his size meant he was not Anak [the famed Giant humans of the Heaven Wars] or of the Floresiensis Race [miniature Oriental humans of the Pleistocene]. His complexion meant he was not of the Idaltu Black Race of Africa, Heidelberg, brown Race of Western Europe or Gribaldi black race of southern Europe. So, he was, most likely, a Cro-Magnon man [found from Europe to Middle East], Neanderthal hybrid [found from

Europe to Middle East], or possibly, a Denisovan hybrid [found from Middle East up to Northern Asia and down to the Far East]. Certainly, he could have been an Anak hybrid of some kind with the reddish complexion, but as far as I knew, all Anak hybrids had the long head. That was such a strong trait that some of the ancient Egyptians and Peruvians still had long heads 37 hundred years ago. With that decision done, I examined this ancient man and his society a little more. Some facial reconstructions are shown next including races named Heidelberg, Grimaldi, Neanderthal, Idaltu, Denisovan, and Cro-Magnon. While all are similar to modern humans, Conrad was more Cro-Magnon like.

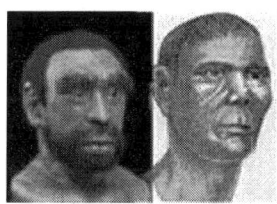

1. He wore somewhat modern looking attire, except for the knee length trousers and no socks.
2. He was civilized and technologically sophisticated.
3. He lived in a house with a table and chairs.
4. He was somewhat emotional when I got in his head.
5. He had a verbal language but I could not figure out what language as I was somehow interpreting his thoughts rather than speaking.
6. He worked in a well commissioned biology lab of some kind.
7. Lastly, he appeared to be designing modifications of animals.

From my historical- religious studies I knew the many would be saved in a wide assortment of vehicles and quite a few would carry animals with them. Also the miscreation of animal types was addressed as one of the reasons the Pleistocene ended.

Genesis 7:2-3- Noah was told-*Take with you clean animals and abominable animals to keep them alive **throughout the earth***.

Of course Noah didn't go throughout the world but he saved some while Moses told us 7 times only things that remained on land would be destroyed.

Genesis 6:17- everything that is on the land shall die-7:4- I will destroy from the face of the earth all living things. :21- all flesh died that moved on the land: everything on the land.-:22-all that was on the dry land died. :23- He destroyed all things which were on the ground. They were destroyed from the land.

In India and Egypt we find images of animals being saved on boats and descriptions of animals on boats is found often.

Others were saved as recorded in the 80-thousand historical references about surviving the flood around the world. Most in boats but some by other means.

***Judeo-Christian - "Enoch 74:15**-I saw likewise the Flying Ship running in the world above to the gates in which the stars turn, which never set. One of these is greater than all which goes around the world.* **Generations of Adam** *-Timnor built great machines of his contriving, his people flew through the air like birds.*

Egyptian- Emerald Text *– [Just before destruction] Gathered I then my people and entered the great ship. Upward we rose into the morning. Suddenly over our home rose the waters. It vanished from Earth --Deep beneath the rocks, I buried my spaceship. Over the spaceship, I erected a marker in the form of*

<u>a lion and man</u>. **Pyramid Texts-** *"During Zep Tepi [Pleistocene], flying gods flew through the air in flying boats[4]*

Americas-Pre-Mayan-*"Chilam Balam" states, "People arriving from the sky on flying ships-they fly above the spheres and reach the stars - "Behold Maya aloft in a circular chariot, 12 thousand cubits in circumference and able to reach the stars."***Pre-Inca***"- the goddess Orejona landed in a great ship from the sky.*

In India Flying ships were called Vimana, others were called Villaxi, others were called flying canoes, but the main thing is when the Pleistocene extinction occurred, only those who got in exotic vehicles survived it. I know my new "friend was going to face the end of the world and I wasn't sure what I was supposed to do about it.

To all the details of these works, Dr. Cindy said, *"I had no idea all of this was in ancient Biblical texts.",* then she said, *"Why did I not know this?"*

To show her other confirming documents as well, I told her, *"The same details could be found everywhere. Besides all of these cross references, I was able to see it first-hand."* Then I continued.

I knew the modifying of animals was a bad thing, but should I warn Conrad about the risks of modifying DNA and the anger that God had towards the modified creations?" My feeling right then was that I should not change history even if I could and besides, if I really wanted to do what would be a good thing, I should be warning our genetics engineers of today.

Poor Whale

---

4 **Pyramid Texts-***These 4000 columns of Hieroglyphic writings were determined to have been written around 5,000 years ago by alignment of the host building to critical star patterns*

As I lay on my bed at Sammy's home, I thought about the UNCLEAN, manufactured Blue Whale with a brain 10 times the size of our current brain. He was locked in a horribly restrictive body that could never leave the ocean. I felt great sadness for their plight knowing that each meal would be limited by massive baleen protrusions that only allowed tiny shrimp to be <u>continuously</u> eaten to keep this huge and smart animal alive. I knew it was not Conrad's fault. It was scientific curiosity that would cause development of the "unclean animals" and the re-animation of Dinosaurs. As a Biological Anthropologist, I immediately wondered if I could find out what animals were being created and how they were doing the recreations and modifications. Not to do it, but just to know the technology. I laid in bed for a long time wondering how I would better communicate with Conrad in the morning. I had no idea how horribly I had offended my close ally, Sammy."

I lost track of time as I usually did and Cindy was looking droopy. I apologized, paid for the meal, got her coat and we left. I took her to her car and she said she really had a great time and thanked me for sharing such intimate details. She also told me she wanted to learn more. But it would not be like a formal session. She just wanted to understand me better.

I told her I had a great time and asked if Saturday would be good. We agreed on a time and she left. Now I was really worried. I didn't know how I was going to continue as things began to get complicated. I didn't even know if I should ever tell someone about these dark secrets, but I was tearing myself up and I really needed to talk to someone. I quickly found out that someone should not have been Sammy.

Sammy the Kurd

As Saturday came. I set up a third meeting with Dr. Cindy and met her at a zoo, of all places. Before I got into memory dump mode, we went through the various encounters and I bored her with my descriptions of various animal groups and phyla. She was ready for business and brought her computer to write notes and comments and I brought mine, just in case. Once we found a quiet place to sit and talk, I continued my story. This part was painful as I continued from my previous detail.

"I knew Sammy was a Kurdish Muslim, but I had no concept of his belief in Jinns and demons and what his people viewed as sacrilege against the moon goddess Allat' or as she is now known, Allah', after Mohammed "allowed" her to be worshipped as a male. I found Sammy on a small carpet with his face to the ground reciting part of the Koran I had never heard before. After a few minutes, he took out a massive knife and began yelling for me, "a devil", to leave his home. His wife was crying and his young son was holding onto his mom's leg. I quickly got all my things and left. Luckily, it was daytime so I went into town to a motel-ish like place I knew, but I found that my notoriety had quickly spread in the small community of Urfa. It was impossible to stay, so I loaded up my belongings, sent the stone article back in a secondary shipment and, finally, boarded a plane coming home. I have to admit I had a tear or two in my red eyes as I decided I had better learn more about sensitivities of religious people around the world if I was ever to need their assistance."

"I decided right then to never let anyone in on what I was actually doing. I still wrote papers on my discoveries and many were not accepted by the main stream anthropological groups, but I was gaining a following with abstract and conspiracy sensitive groups and, so far, the University had not cancelled my teaching opportunities."

"That's why I came to you in the first place," I told Cindy. My boss brought me to you and I needed the job.

Cindy stopped me there and said, *"I can't believe you have never told anyone about your gift besides Sammy. What you can do is a gift from God and it could help mankind."*

Just her saying others should hear about what I can do made me shutter and I knew I would have to explain just how close I came to not being here, but that would be for another time. She continued and said, *"You are the J-man, aren't you?"* I laughed, but it really wasn't that funny.

I continued my story. *"As I got home and finally got the stone purse out of customs, I went home and placed the artifact on the table. I decided I could not give this artifact to the University so I kept it. There were many other items that I gave up and the University loved what I had brought. I had found many pottery shards, an image of what I believed was the predecessor to Baal, cooking utensils, and even bits of cloth that were all cleared by the office of antiquities, but this one had DNA. By the way, no one knew why the Pleistocene and Early Holocene rulers and "scientists" carried these ridiculous "purses" around with them everywhere."* I quickly pulled out my trusty laptop next to hers and showed her some of the more well-known images of Pleistocene and Early Holocene Man-purses being carried everywhere. At this point I also wondered about the fish outfit.

"Sometimes the purse carriers dressed up in fish outfits, but everyone that was anyone, ALWAYS carried his purse. This might be why there was DNA on Conrad's purse," I told her.

Later, I would find out that these purses first were symbolic of the gathering of the fruit of the tree-of-life that allowed everyone to live extremely long times.

"Yes, there was such a fruit, and all the people I met were well over 500 years old; even Conrad," I interjected; but the solid stone purses were carried in remembrance of what they had lost when the "fruit tree of life" was lost, sort of an exercise device for the elite, and an object to show status, like a really heavy Rolex watch. Later, Conrad would tell me the only reason he had one of the ridiculous things was to make a pilgrimage to Gobekli. He told me he dropped the thing and it fell in a hole so

he thought it was a sign and left it behind, even though it had cost quite a bit to have it made. He then stated he had only worshipped our creator described by Noah since he returned home.

As soon as I got a chance to "intermingle" with Conrad, I sat at home, rubbed my purse, and soon, I was seeing what he was seeing 10 to 12 thousand years ago. Unfortunately, I found there were some things I could not control. The main thing was "when".

Here I was, inside this man. Conrad said *"Friend"* when I focused on it and then he/me told himself *"From 10 thousand years in future"*. *"Time travel by my lifeforce"*.

I was shocked when Conrad introduced himself and began talking to me. Then he said, *"Are you the same person who came to me 2 years ago"*.

For me it had been a couple of days, but the time link was to people not time. I hoped that even if I could not control when that it would at least push me forward in time for Conrad. I told him I was the same guy and he immediately started telling me about his world with excitement. He didn't even seem very upset that I had invaded his mind; had made him think he was crazy; and all the rest. Conrad was excited about talking to someone from the future. At first, he was asking me questions that I could answer yes or no. *"Are you a Biologist?" "Do you "gene splice" animals in your world?" "Are males dominant?" "Do you believe in the Creator God?" "Do you still have sex?"* but soon the questions became harder to answer. *"What planets do you live on?" "What is your main power source and how is it distributed?"* Unbelievably, I soon could almost talk to Conrad like I would another person. I can't exactly explain how my "Talking" happened, but we had detailed conversations.

Gene Splicing

After telling him that we certainly have sex and that women's equality was popular in my day, I sadly informed him that fewer and fewer believe in our creator every year. I then explained how we are gene splicing in an attempt to reconstruct the Mammoths that will be extinct in the future and that we are modifying animals to grow human organs for retrieval and human patient replacements. I told him of the experimental construction of eyes on the knees of fruit-flies, and how we modified chickens to have no feathers to make cooking easier.

Conrad came back with, *"I love to fly over the massive herds of Mammoths, Unicorns, and Rhinos. They don't even care. You could probably jump on one, but I never did."* I had to go back and investigate unicorns as I thought they were some type of weird horses, but reading the Bible I quickly found I had been misinformed.

Numbers 23-24*God - He hath - <u>strength of a unicorn</u>: he shall - break their bones*

Deuteronomy 33:17-*his <u>horns are like the horns of unicorns</u>: <u>with them he shall push the people to the ends of the earth</u>:*

Job 39:9-10-*Will the unicorn be willing to serve you? <u>Canst you bind the unicorn</u>?*

Isaiah 34:7-*And <u>the unicorns shall come down</u> with them, and the bullocks with the bulls;*

It was evident the Bible was talking about an animal called a Siberian Unicorn that was bigger and stronger than the Mammoth or Rhino. Sometimes called Elasmotherium, Moses just called it a unicorn because it had this massive singular horn. I was jealous of Conrad's view of the huge herds of these mighty beasts. Of course, the Unicorn was not the largest grazing animal of that time. The massive Taper-like beast was twice as large as the unicorn, but he was apparently very docile.

I showed Cindy, and now you guys, a size comparison of the various herd animals Conrad had seen.

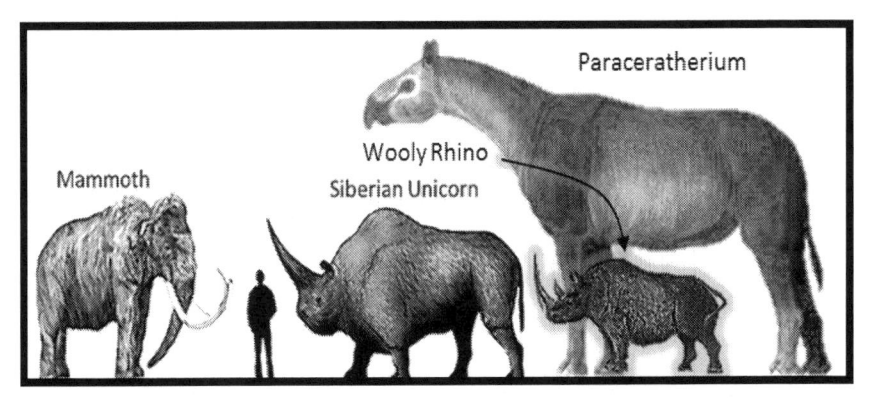

[Figure: Size comparison showing Mammoth, Wooly Rhino / Siberian Unicorn, and Paraceratherium, with a human silhouette for scale.]

Then he said, *"We routinely manufacture animals. One company in the East wanted large chickens. I modified a chicken to produce an egg that was huge. It ended up with very long legs and neck and it could no longer fly, but the company wanted it for eggs and meat."* Conrad then showed me some of his creations which were now pets living in his home. One was a cross between a Cat and a Bat. While the wings weren't strong enough for flight, the cat could glide from the roof to the ground and not get hurt. As he was telling me, I remembered that many cats have been born with vestigial wings and now I knew why! —As I continued, I showed Dr. Cindy a few of the many winged cats who must have, at one time, bred with Conrad's modification.

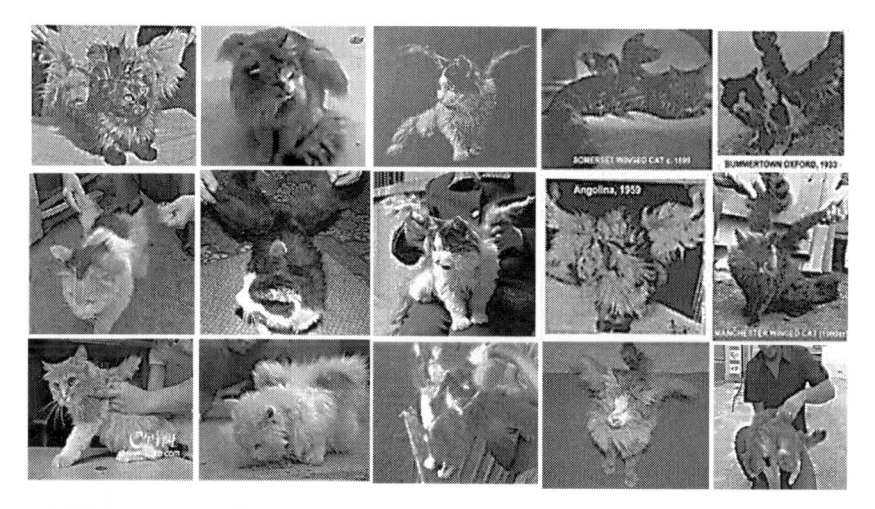

I told him we call that new chicken an Ostrich in my time and that some cats are still born with wings. This gave Conrad a sense of pride that his work would be remembered in some way. He also told me, *"We also, routinely, manufacture organs from patients' own defective organs and we have accelerated the growth of most to a very short time to allow for reasonable replacements. I would say most of us have had at least one organ replaced."* He showed me a scar from his liver replacement. *"These critical discoveries and designs are being done every week by our team.*

Horrible Anak Humans

"When I was younger," he continued, *"there simply was no way to produce enough meat to satisfy the cravings of the horrible Giants and some engaged in selective human sacrifice to those who would call themselves gods. Many times, the one who was sacrificed was an innocent girl. Let me tell you there were rumors of the girls being brutally molested before finally being eaten. If we had not invented ways to greatly increase the available sources of meat, I fear we would have all died to the marauders.*

It was no wonder Conrad held so much hate for those who now had forced the entire world into a thousand-years of an almost continuous series of wars. Almost every ancient text about the Anak giants describe horrors against the normal sized people and they end the same as our creator ensured that only 10 percent of them escaped the upcoming end of the Pleistocene and I told Conrad so.

Electricity and Oil

After calming Conrad down a little, I explained about how we generate electricity from a wide assortment of methods and use oil to power our vehicles.

He came back and said. *"There are a number of fuel sources in my world. The main one was located in Egypt and was a massive pyramid structure. The structure was actually an electrical power source that generated alternating electro-magnetic transmissions that were tuned to the resonance of the earth so the ground would appear to be a very low resistance."* I had already read the theories on how electricity was developed in what we call the Great Pyramid and read how the Egyptian King, Thoth, built the structure during the Pleistocene, but this was great affirmation.

Conrad then said, *"Power storage areas around the world collected the valuable commodity. We pull electricity in directly from Egypt, and a major remote storage facility was in the western continent [I knew he was talking about America]."* I determined it must have been the Mica-walled Temple to the Sun in the ancient city we call Teotihuacan, near present day Mexico City. Only now are investigators understanding the complexity of this storage-sister to what we call the Great Pyramid.

He continued by stating, *"The second most common source of energy for our homes and machines in areas that cannot pull electricity directly was by Nuclear reaction steam turbines. Areas outside the cities, must rely on this secondary method as they do not have the equipment to transfer Egyptian energy.* He continued by explaining, *"A large number of nuclear processing areas in Africa were developed to process fissionable material and several large power plants were located at critical areas including a large one in the southern Americas."*

I explained to my doctor, *"I had read about the 16 pre-Pleistocene Nuclear processing modules in Gabon, Africa that were found to be missing major amounts of processed fuel, but this was real confirmation of their use and what appears to be a well-guarded PreInca nuclear electrical plant had been found at the site Sacsayhauman, Peru, but details of what the protected area was used for has been a mystery. I couldn't believe how he had solved some of the strangest mysteries of the world in one paragraph."*

The last method Conrad indicated was chemical discharge batteries (of which we have found remains around the world). *"While we use many different chemicals, for our vehicles,"* he said, *"We mostly use cinnabar crystals that are melted to release high energy Mercury for the chemical discharge."* (The cinnabar/mercury crystals were depicted often in Sumerian and Indian literature for flying vehicles.) He also told me, *"The poor people use oil instead of electricity for lighting, but I am in a better position."*

Cindy stopped me a minute and said, *"I'm sorry but what in the world are you talking about. What in the world are you saying about the Great Pyramid, Atlantis, cinnabar engines, flying machines and their understanding of those esoteric sciences. This sounds crazy!"*

I said the only thing that came to my mind, when she said that, *"Of course it sounds crazy, our schools hide the truth. They hide the evidence and they don't want to go against predecessor quasi-scientists that were probably protecting their predecessor scientific leaders. This makes my job as an Archeologist much more difficult; especially when I know the truth and I must "soften" the consensus line so I don't lose my job."*

I showed the Pyramidic Electricity machine schematic to Cindy, so she would know what Conrad was stating. I told her, *"The machine that built up electricity that Conrad was talking about was integrated into what is now wrongly called Khufu's Pyramid."* I explained that a number of researchers are beginning to understand how the thing worked, by using 5 massive red granite oscillating crystals; the pressure of the stones above it to compress the granite, an impressive baffle system; and entry ports to place acid and base materials to initiate internally controlled explosions once the machine was started. All the Egyptians had to do was to periodically pour the acid and base into the massive machine and it, almost magically, supplied AC electricity for the entire region.

Here is the drawings I showed her and if you are interested in how the machine worked there are a number of similar theories. Almost all suggest this strange pyramidic structure produced electricity. I know some suggest aliens from outer space made it, but there is written testimony that Thoth was the designer and builder, during the Pleistocene.

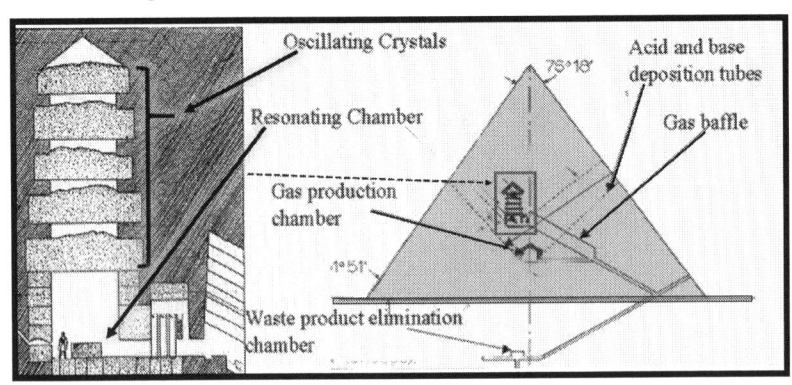

Electricity Sent to America

I didn't have many images in my laptop, but I pulled up images of what many believe to be the ancient Sacsayhauman Peruvian Nuclear power plant that had been well protected thousands of years ago and showed her what was known. If someone wanted to get near the Nuclear Power Plant, they had to traverse 3 massive sets of 20-foot-high walls that were placed progressively up the emplacement of the circular containment area with no doors and 3-foot thick walls. The collage also shows a modern nuclear-containment-building in Russia that was not nearly as protected [lower right]. I also explained that the Pleistocene civilization had been at an advanced state of technology for 30 thousand years while we have only been out of our last Bronze Age for about 4 thousand years. I said, *"Just image what our society would be like in another 20 thousand years or so."*

I then explained, *"This was the most protected area of all of the PreIncan Kingdom and it must have supplied energy for many hundreds or even thousands of years."*

Cindy, seemed to calm down a little, but she did shake her head a few times as she tried to wrestle with these new possibilities so I continued.

"Conrad began expounding on his gene splicing, and creation of a wide variety of animal components that could be used to replace organs of the older people and war victims. He indicated he had recently transferred to a section that reconstructed the ancient dinosaurs and supplied them as exhibits in zoos, and he had actually built a number of animals that exceeded the capabilities of the original ones. As he began explaining about the excitement he had in creation, he very quickly stopped, turned around, and began talking about God and gods. He wanted me to know he didn't think he was a god just because he knew about gene splicing and he didn't think the giant scientists [Anak humans] who developed the processes were gods either."

Anak Were Not Gods

Conrad continued by saying, *"Many of the ancient giant people had begun believing they were like gods and normal sized people, my size, began treating them like gods."* (I knew from my studies, the people he was talking about were the ones called Anak, in Biblical history).

He sadly told me he was not one of those who believed ancient people were gods, but the numbers of believers continue to rise. He stopped and asked me if the Creator God still talks to humans like he did to the great Enoch? I tried to explain as best I could about God his incarnation as a man named Jesus, but he, evidently, had heard it before from a man named Noah, who heard it from his great-grand father Enoch. When he told me those 2 names, I almost couldn't contain myself and Conrad knew my feelings as if I was inside him.

His Friend "Noah"

"Then he asked me something fantastic. You are not even going to believe this!" I said as I jumped out of my chair and came over close to Dr. Cindy.

Conrad said, *"Would like to visit Noah? We have to go visit Noah while you are here, he yelled and jumped around. I was going to bring his a crate of nails for his masterpiece, anyway."* He called his wife and said, *"We are going on a trip to Shulon."* She was excited. It seems she and Norea, Noah's wife, were good friends. Just then, I wondered just how old Conrad and Maria were. The Bible indicated when the Flood came, Noah was almost 600 jubilee-years-old, and his wife, Norea was 60-jubilee-years older than him. I looked up jubilees and found out they were associated with 7-year periods, so Noah was already really old.

I asked Conrad how old he was and he told me he was 490 jubilee-years-old. For a moment I was shocked, but in studying Egyptian, Babylonian, Sumerian, and Assyrian histories, their kings all live much longer than Noah so I decided Conrad was Middle-Aged. This started to make more sense when I read in the books *"Adam and Eve I and II"* that Adam lived 5500 'regular' years after Seth, his son, was a grown man so most say Adam lived to be about 6500 years old which makes his 'creation' about 37 thousand years ago which is identical to the date the Cro-Magnon humans just appeared in the Pleistocene and in complete agreement with *II Esdras 14,* in the King James Bible, and the Adam and Eve books of earlier Bibles and multiple copies of these books were found in the Essene libraries that would have been used by Jesus and the early Christians to understand how God created man.

I would later find that, not only would I live with Conrad for a while, but also, I would have very close relationships with his close "friends", their wives, and their children. The children part would take some explaining. At this point I showed my dear doctor a sketch I had done of the Pleistocene men that would teach me about how to care about people deeply while helping me understand how the Pleistocene ended and humanity survived. They looked like healthy versions of us, with similar facial hair, mannerisms, and even the clothing didn't seem very strange. Even when I saw Noah and his family, they were very similar except for one unusual trait. They were all barefooted and had somewhat longer hair.

[Sketch of six men labeled: Duke, Marlin, Bartlet, Jothan, Reese, Conrad]

I'll get to all the others as we go along. Conrad looked kind of like the image to the right. Short cropped reddish colored hair. I would have shown you reader's what Methuselah, Lamech, Noah, his wife Norea, Shem, and his wife, Mary, looked like from another sketch, but Cindy now has it in her living room framed, so you will just have to take my word on their looks. They all had dark reddish hair and they had fairly light reddish skin. The men had no facial hair and Noah looked to be the strongest of the bunch, but I'm getting ahead of myself as this adventure made me understand the details of the Biblical accounts so that I could read through various versions and interpret a closer truth. Noah would just be the first step. I have to admit if I had legs when Conrad suggested the visit, I would have been jumping up and down just like Conrad did. Not only would I talk to the savior of the Adamics and many, many animals, but I might get to visit with his dad Lamech, and Grandfather Methuselah [the oldest Cro-Magnon to ever live. On the sad side, I knew he and Lamech would both die just before the Extinction flood. Methuselah was recorded as living to be 969-jubilee-years or almost 7 thousand years old, but I was told the Anak giants lived even longer in most cases.

Seeing Noah

Before I get to this, let me say, I think part of my job is to provide a saner image of those who lived during different times. I was truly stoked. Conrad told me, Noah lived in the next kingdom. This may have given me more clues about who Conrad was and where we were. I had believed we were in Turkey, but it seems we were probably in Pakistan, Afghanistan or Iraq, as Adam's Kingdom of Shulon was just east of Eden on a large plateau that most, now, believe was in Central Iran.

Conrad and his wife, Maria, got in a strange vehicle that could only hold 4 friendly people, but what it lacked in size in made up for in something else. We lifted off the ground and we were on our way. The vehicle was quiet and comfortable. I could hear some type of "brrrr" like and electric plasma discharge and I saw a greenish glow out the back, but I had very little feeling of motion. Conrad's wife looked over at him and asked, *"Is that guy from the future with you?"* Conrad told her I was there and she introduced herself simply as Conrad's wife and quickly said, *"What do women do in the future, how do they dress, do they have the freedoms of males?"* My answer was, *"They do anything they want, wear what they want, and have the same privilege!"* I added, *"They love shoes!"* She continued with many other questions about entertainment, food, places, if I had children, what was my training in; and on and on. She asked me if I could invade others. I told her I didn't know so she said, *"Try me!"* Conrad placed his hand on her shoulder and immediately I could feel and sense her almost like I had been doing with Conrad. As Conrad removed his hand, I told her about how she was feeling, what her likes and dislikes were, and how she hated the wars and the Anak rulers. She said *"Wow!*

You are a strange future man," and then she giggled. We were quiet for a time and Conard pointed out some of the beautiful mountains and waterfalls below. Then, Maria reached over and hugged Conrad and said, *"I'm glad you are here,"* then she exclaimed, *"What about sex?"* --

Saved By Shulon

Luckily, we were already near the community of the Adamic people and Conrad explained, *"This land, called Shulon, on top of a huge plateau, is ruled by the holy man, Lamech, who was the 6-great grandson of Adam the first of the Adamic people. Adam was also father of Timnor who was my 5-Great grandfather, but we have always lived in the land of Hanar."*

"Conrad indicated all of the people living in Shulon were from the lineage of Methuselah who is extremely old. He said the great Enoch was Methuselah's father and Lamech is Methuselah's son. Then he quickly said, *"The man you really should meet is the one called Noah. You just have got to see his floating craft. He has been working on it for over 5 years and it is still not completely finished as he does not allow electrical equipment up here to help the construction. He says it distracts him from God."*

Conrad added hesitantly, *"Besides building the ship, Noah, has been busy warning everyone about the upcoming end of the world."*

I didn't say anything about that to him as I wasn't sure what I should say. From the Jewish Essene book *"Generations of Adam"* I showed my doctor the lineage of Cain's kingdom, the kingdom of Shulon and that of Hanar that was verified by Conrad. Then I went back to the details of my trip. It's the next graphic for those reading the book.

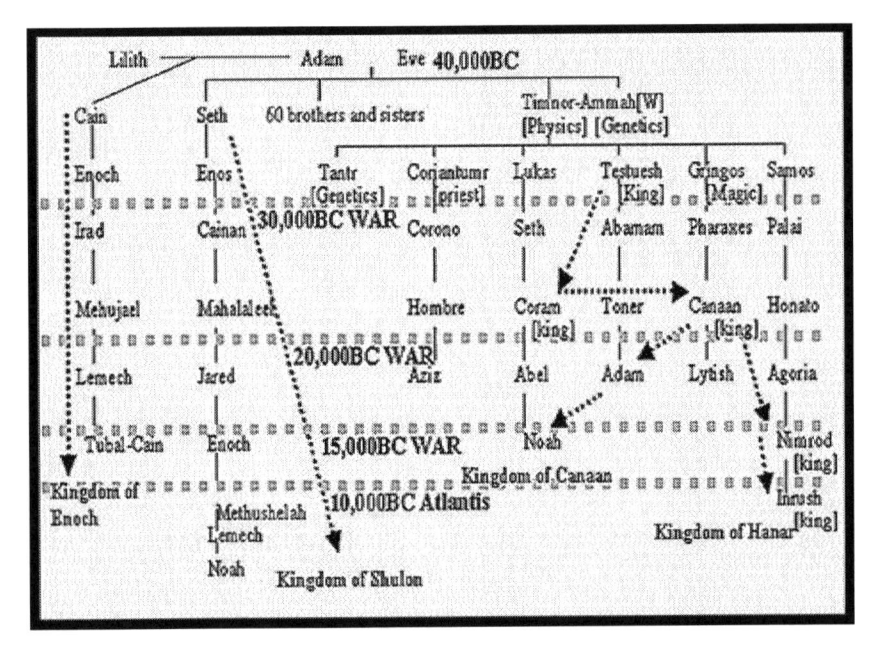

```
         Lilith ─────────── Adam , Eve 40,000BC
                            ┌─────────┴─────────┐
   ┌Cain      Seth    60 brothers and sisters   Timnor-Ammah[W]
                                                [Physics] [Genetics]
   Enoch     Enos ·.    Tantr    Conjantumr  Lukas   Testuesh  Gringos  Samos
                      (Genetics)   [priest]         [King]    [Magic]
   Irad      Cainan ·.30,000BC WAR  Corono    Seth    Abamam  Pharaxes  Palai
   Mehujael  Mahalaleel              Hombre   Coram   Toner   Canaan   Honato
                                              [king]                  [king]
   Lemech    Jared    ·.20,000BC WAR           Abel    Adam   Lytish   Agoria
                                      Aziz
   Tubal-Cain  Enoch    ·.15,000BC WAR         Noah                    Nimrod
                                                                       [king]
  Kingdom of                        Kingdom of Canaan                  Inrush
     Enoch    Methushelah ·.10,000BC Atlantis                          [king]
              Lemech                           Kingdom of Hanar
              Noah    Kingdom of Shulon
```

Cindy stopped me in mid thought and said, *"Are you talking about the actual Lamech and Noah who were the descendants of Adam from the Bible and took all the animals in the Ark?"*

"The one and only!" I exclaimed.

Backing up to an earlier comment, she came back with, *"What was this reference to sex?"*

I told her I wasn't sure I could discuss that part, but the Doctor immediately said, *"It will be fine. There is no need to be embarrassed."*

With a silent chuckle, I had to tell her, *"It's not that. It was a massive shock and what happened later was out of my control and almost too exotic for me to even describe as their customs were somewhat different."* Dr. Cindy had no comeback, so I continued.

"While the city where Conrad lived looked modern, multi-story buildings, nice homes with carpeting and manicured yards; the place where the Adamic people lived looked comfortable, but more like a copy of an Amish village. They had cobblestone streets and horse and buggies were used. They, evidently, had rejected the modern conveniences, but I could feel a warmth and great friendliness from all the descendants of Adam who had remained. The first man we saw was Lamech, but a number of the citizens came over with him. Lamech was the old and wise father of Noah, I wished I had refreshed my memory of the books *"Genesis", "Generations of Adam" and "Adam and Eve"* before coming."

At first, I could not understand Lamech, but after he talked awhile, I, somehow, could understand his language just as I did Conrad. Lamech asked Conrad about the wars below the plateau of Shulon where all the pure Cro-Magnon people called Adamics lived. All Adamics were warned not to mix with the children of Cain, but a large number had left even during the time of Seth and this exodus continued through rule of Lamech, Adam's son to the 6th generation. Even Noah's own daughters had left the plateau. Those who had not married outsiders lived, worked, and praised the creator on the plateau that would later become a major part of Iran. I had read about Noah's daughter named Birren and her husband Bitheus, but I decided I wouldn't bring it up unless Noah did.

Conrad told him about several of his friends or relatives that had died in the fighting and indicated that even the capitol city in Hanar had been "burned to the ground" I could see Lamech had known some of the victims and was very sad. Then Conrad said something bad about the "giants"- I could feel hate and loathing. I assumed he was talking about the Anak Giants. These power-hungry people had been described as the instigators of what would become a worldwide horror according to a number of the ancient Essene writings as I found out later. No wonder Conrad and those nearby had such disdain for these overlords.

Conrad explained to Lamech what he understood of the present circumstance so Lamech began talking directly to me. He asked about the "future world" wars, numbers of people living, and similar questions Conrad had already asked, but then he got somber and asked how many would survive the upcoming end of the world? Through Conrad, I explained that about 10% of the Anak people, a significant number of hybrid gentiles from around the world, and a group of the descendants of Adam. I almost told him only 8-Adamics would survive, but I just could not.

Conrad explained that his family and a group of believers were preparing a large flying ship to escape the predicted worldwide flood and that Lamech's son was preparing a massive boat to carry animals to safety. He said he knew of a massive flying colony that orbited the Earth and he believed the Anak would seek shelter there. Through Conrad, I asked Lamech about how many of Adam's descendants were on the plateau. Sadly, Lamech said there were only 33 who had not gone down the mountain to the Land of Cain and the Anak." Conrad explained of himself [to me] that he was not one of those of the Land of Cain whose Kingdom was laughingly called the "Kingdom of Enoch" [the name of Cain's first son]. He quickly explained again that he lived in the Kingdom of Hanar where there were still a number of followers of the God of Lamech.

"I already knew Lamech would die in the Pleistocene Wars and his dad, Methuselah, would also die just before the upcoming flood as described in the book of Genesis, and I knew Noah would take his children to safety along with as many animals as he could pack in his huge ship, but what I saw was not what I expected. Noah had a close-cropped beard and fairly short hair. In fact, all of the pure Cro-Magnon/Adamics had a similar hair style and all the women had long hair and no beard. All the people looked like they were 30 to 40 years old and I knew Noah had to be at least 550 jubilee years old."

"Noah, evidently, had seen Conrad's flying machine and stopped his work to come visit a minute. When I saw Noah coming up from his almost complete ship I was awe-stuck like he was a movie star or something. From what I could see, he had hired almost a hundred workers - all cutting sawing, rigging, and building. As he left, they continued to work as he came to see what was going on. His sons and their wives must have stayed with the Ark, but Noah was with his bride, the daughter of Methuselah, who, I knew to be Norea. I was so excited to talk to the one who would save humanity, I, sort of, made Conrad run towards the most well-known of the Pleistocene men and his wife. Noah, called for Conrad to stop and asked him why he was so excited. By this time, Conrad had reached Noah and told him the running part wasn't him. He introduced me and I hugged him and Norea."

"I could feel the fear Noah had. He wondered if he should be the one to continue humanity or not. His anger got the best of him too often and he had not stood up to those of his brothers, sisters, and cousins who had left the plateau, enticed by the naked men and women and the musicians of Cain's Kingdom below the plateaued plain."

Noah looked at me through Conrad, and asked, *"How do you know me in the future?"*

I told him, *"You are one of the most famous men in all of history. Millions know your name, your journey, and all about you---10 thousand years from now."*

Noah said, *"I don't understand?"*

As I had done with Maria, I was able to project my soul to Noah, so long as Conrad held onto Noah's arm. This gave all three of us a great intimacy. In the broad sense of things, we all became the same entity. I like to think of it as me "becoming Noah" for a short time. In this state, I explained directly to Noah how he was the only one who could continue the pure race and how God would one day incarnate himself through his lineage, how our creator God had chosen him from his birth to carry the Adamic line into the next Age, and how his descendants would make a great nation, and that he would be remembered for his devotion for many, many centuries. I explained how his children would be very important in the repopulation of the world and God would take him safely through the horrors that were to come.

He felt so very guilty that no one was able to go with him except those selected by God, but Conrad assured him that those who continued the faith in Hanar would be fine and they had another plan for escape. Noah, asked me one thing that I was pretty sure he would ask.

Noah asked, *"Do you know if my daughters survived the Flood?"*

I let him know truthfully, *"I read a number of documents describing your daughter Birren, her husband Bitheus, and their 3 sons, Adna, Bath, and Ladra, and daughter Cessair. They all survived."*

Noah said, *"My wife and I both thank you for that detail and hope.—What were my grandchildren's names again?"* I said, *Your grandsons were Adna, Bath, and Ladra, and Ladra married his sister, Cessair. I do not know what children they may have had."* Both Norea and Noah were hugging and Norea even gave Noah a kiss at this news.

Cindy stopped me and said, *"I thought Noah only had three sons, Shem, Ham and Japheth?"*

I told her, *"Noah's daughter Birren was one of around 3 daughters who married outside the Adamic line and had to find a different way to come through the worldwide flood. Birren had gone down to the kingdom of Cain and had married a man named Bitheus. Luckily, I had a substantial Irish heritage and new of the stories of Noah's Daughter and son-in-law."*

As with the other questions, I pulled up a couple of short texts to reduce her concerns. The first was from the Biblical histories and the second was confirmation from ancient Scottish historians. Here they are, in case you had questions.

Bible-Genesis Apocryphon 6[5]- *Then, Noah's wife conceived and bore him three sons <u>and several daughters</u>. I then took wives from my brother's family for my sons, and <u>I gave my daughters to my nephews</u> according to the law ordained to the sons of man.*

According to a large number of thousand year old histories, Noah's daughter, Birren, married an outsider, Bitheus, and could not go with the others on the Arc. According to historical records, after Noah, would not allow her and her sisters in the "Holy" ship. She, her sons, and daughter were all saved another way, probably by God's hand.

Annals of the Four Masters *-"Bith gathered up his children including his sons Adna, Bath, and Ladra his wife Birren and his daughter Cessair, and as fast as they could go northward they left with them were 2 other men named Fintan and Ladra and 50 other women..-Desperately, Bitheus gathered up his children including his sons Adna, Bath, his wife <u>Birren [assumed to be the daughter of Noah],</u> and his daughter Cessair. They left as fast as they could go northward. With them were 2 other men named Fintan and Ladra and 50 other women. In Ireland the 3 men and 50 women split up. Bith took 25 women and headed for*

---

[5] **"Genesis Apocryphon",** *believed to have been the source texts for the books called Jasher and Genesis only fragments were found in the Nazarene Christian library known as the Dead Sea Scrolls. While genesis is in all Bibles, Jasher is only found in the Ethiopian, Essene, and Syriac Bibles today but it is mentioned in 2 places of the other Bibles.*

the tallest mountain, Carrauntoohil, which reached 2/3 of a mile in the sky.[6]

***Book of Leinster*[7] 26** *Cessair and her dad, Bith, son of Noah took Ireland, forty days before the Flood. Cessair came from the East, the woman was daughter of Bith;*

Once Birren and Bitheus got to Ireland, they rode out the axis shift, following storm, and worldwide flood, 8000 BC. Very little is known about them after the flood, but, at least some survived.

"Noah asked me a hundred questions and I asked him just as many. It wasn't that I had not asked many questions of Conrad, himself, but I was talking to Noah. He asked about his grandkids. I quoted what I remembered the details from two books about how many grandchildren he would have- *"from Japheth 460, from Shem 300, from Ham 730, and you will have 30 additional children."* Norea looked at Noah with a stern face as Conrad spoke the number 30. I went to a different topic to remember what Noah was like as a boy and young man with Lamech filling his heart with love.

Jasher 7: 9-20- *The sons of Japheth were about four hundred and sixty men. The <u>sons of Ham were **about** seven hundred and thirty men</u>. The sons of Shem were about three hundred men. --*

---

[6] *"Annals of the Four Masters"- is one of several Irish histories first written about a thousand years ago which show how Scythians and Egyptians conquered Ireland and knew Moses It is made up of 7 volumes-complied around 1635 AD and it reviews history from the Deluge until 1616 AD*

[7] ***Book of Leinstar*** *or Lebar Na Nuachongbala, written in Celtic, author unknown included a collection of ancient poems from between 457 and 1189 AD. Transcribed into Irish in the 12th century. This contains the history of Ireland from the Time of Adam.*

***"History of Babylonia"*-** in that book Noah had 30 additional children born after the Deluge.

Noah was giggling when I told him about him having additional kids, but I'm not sure about the look Norea gave me. He wanted to go tell his kids right away, but I said maybe that is a topic for another time, as it might be a shock to their wives, you know.

He also said, *"I hope Birren will be so blessed."* "He asked me about wars." I told him, *"There was no indication of any major war after the flood for over 4 thousand years."*

"Then, strangely he asked when the incarnate God would return to the world."

I told him, *"He would come in all his splendor about 8 thousand years after the flood."*

On and on he went and Norea stepped in and told him to slow down or Conrad was going to faint.

Conrad shot up and said, *"Don't worry about me, I'm learning just as much as you husband."*

"I had hoped Conrad and I helped give him the confidence Noah needed to take on the burden of the entire world. I don't know if it helped a great deal, but I think he greatly appreciated the encouragement and after talking a short time and Noah showing me the great craft that would bring so many to safety, he left us and went back to his continuing work. I could even see he was beginning to fill sections of the ship with supplies."

As Conrad [me], Maria, and Lamech went back to the central area of the village where our transportation was, I wanted to get to know Lamech a little better and Conrad touched his arm.

It was evident Lamech knew he would die in the godforsaken wars that had been escalating for years and he was troubled by the whole mess, but he was so very proud of Noah. Like Noah, he thought it was his fault that so many of those from Shulon left the plateau to live with the daughters of Cain and the Anak. I told him that their decisions could not be changed by him. He was a holy man and part of the reason Noah was able to continue what he had been assigned to do, that without his love, no one would survive this mess. I let him understand all those following the ways of God, owed him for that opportunity. I could tell his misery was lessened by that knowledge and he kissed Conrad on the cheek and blessed him and me. Then he said I guess you want to see my father while you are here.

We went down to a small house with smoke coming out of the chimney and inside the one and only Methuselah was sitting in what looked to be a comfortable chair. He had been writing details of his father's life [Enoch], for Noah to take with him on his upcoming journey. Little did he know he would outlive Lamech his son. Conrad greeted him and I entered him as I had done with Lamech. Methuselah was still in awe of his dad, Enoch, and so proud of both Lamech and his grandson, Noah, but like Lamech, he was deeply saddened by the large number who had left and thought he had done something wrong. I told him he was a great man who was ultimately responsible for saving those believing in God's ultimate authority and that without his instruction all this would never have happened. He told me of Enoch and the last time he saw his father as he was simply taken to help God another way. He indicated his dad loved everyone including the Anak who he knew would suffer much as they would not be able to sleep after death. Methuselah knew he would not live to see the Extinction and was good with that. Strangely, the three of us had a short prayer together for Noah's safe travel and Conrad's safety as well. Conrad leaned down and kissed Methuselah on the cheek as Lamech had done and Methuselah fell asleep as was his normal action these days. We left his home and said "bye" to everyone including a number I did not know who would die along with Lamech whenever the people rushed to gain access to Noah's survival craft. They knew what they needed to do and were ready to do it. I could feel both their fear and their faith. Conrad and Maria got back into their vehicle and we left.

"I never thought I would describe that meeting to anyone and now I have spilled my feelings, passion, and internal doubts to you," I said as I noticed the Doc.

Cindy just said, *"I'm so glad you did and I'm so very honored to be the one you confided in. Believe me when I tell you, I think I understand your dilemma. What you can tell everyone would certainly lift them up, but many would title you as a charlatan and evil manipulator so you think you need to stay silent. I promise we will figure out a way for you to live with your amazing capability and be able to continue without tearing yourself and your students apart."*

Filling in Dr. Cindy

Before I went on, I took a little break. I wanted to explain to Cindy about the dilemma of the Adamic people, so I said, *"The information I gave him about having children might have been the best news as I saw no small children in Shulon, in fact, there just weren't many of the Adamics left in Shulon because of nudity."*

"What?" She asked.

"According to just about every ancient Judeo-Christian history, the people of Cain seemed to always be naked, beautiful, and alluring. Additionally, most of the Adamics were too weak to resist. Instead of the kingdom getting larger and larger, most of the people climbed down to get with the naked people living nearby." I showed her a number of texts indicating how bad it really was. Every patriarch from Seth to Noah had one horrible nemesis-nudity. The naked men and women of Cain's group frolicked, played music, and taunted the Adamics all the time. Most of the Adamics left the plateau as described in this snippet, I read to her.

Adam and Eve II- <u>Jarad was told there were things below the mountain that were pure. Jarad went with the "disguised Satan" and was met by MANY women offering themselves to him for sex and pleasure.</u> - ---- *When the Adamics saw that the daughters of Cain were beautiful in form and <u>that they were naked</u>, they became inflamed with lust. And the daughters of Cain defiled their bodies. And when Enoch, Methuselah, Lamech and Noah saw them, their hearts suffered.*

Miscalculated Time

After I was finished with the nakedness problem and Dr. Cindy was through writing another note, I continued. "After the Noah meeting, I knew something important. I had miscalculated the timing. These people were already in the last portion of the massive season of world wars. I knew Noah and his wife were very old. Noah confirmed this when he told me he was 500 "Jubilee" years old when he married his beautiful bride. [That would be about 3500 solar years.] Strangely, they still looked like they were relatively young. One would think that should mean there would be children all around, in fact, I saw very few actual children where Conrad was living."

Almost No Children

"Conrad had told me that whenever the season of wars came along, the number of births had gotten fewer and fewer I remembered the last part of the Pleistocene was called the Younger Dryas. While it was a stupid name of a flower. The evidence associated with the time that I was currently visiting was known for unbelievable changes over a few hundred-year period. Evidence of large amounts of high density carbon microspheres and nano-diamonds that were found around the world showed ultrahigh temperatures associated with massive explosions. High levels of radioactivity found in many Pleistocene animal remains along with the huge number of major human DNA mutations that happened near the end of the Pleistocene showed how horrible the wars would become. As almost ½ of all major human mutations occurred near the end of the Pleistocene, it probably meant high levels of nuclear or other gene damaging radiation was being sensed by the inhabitants as a gift of the massive warring. Reproduction seemed to be affected negatively, in some way.

I showed my doctor, scientist's indicators of the horrors this season of warring left in the ground including massive quantities of spherules, diamonds, and charcoal. Here is one of the graphs showing the indicators of nuclear wars or something very similar as the average world temperature dropped and then shot-up as extinction occurred.

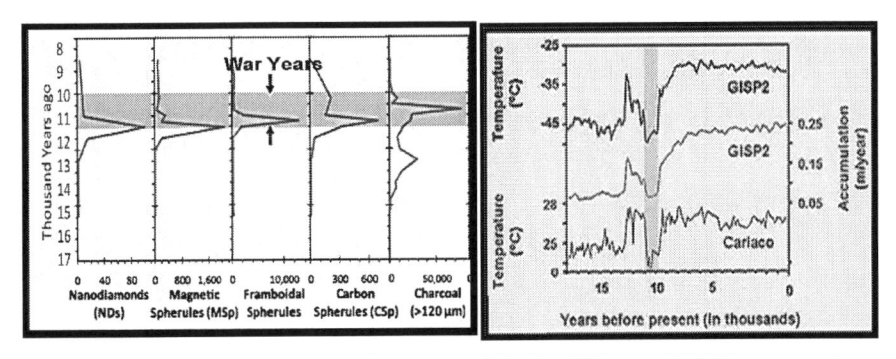

These stressors may have increased infertility as DNA mutations were changing the races of people. Haplotype [DNA mutation] researchers tell us that 12 different races of humans would survive the flood. I showed Cindy how that looked in a graph and the graph is shown next. With ½ of all races spontaneously occurring near the end of the Pleistocene, it is well known that this was a very critical time in human development. Haplotype mutations are abbreviated as letters so we lesser people can trace our race beginnings. My graphic, sort of, shows how each race developed during and just after the Pleistocene.

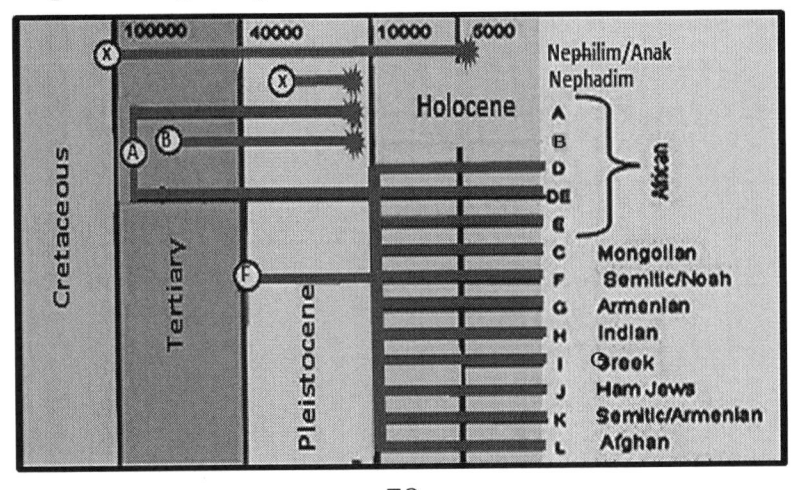

The letters on the graph are called Haplotypes and they describe complex mutations associated with developing different races. Exposure to the war-torn atmosphere was reducing fertility and changing the DNA of those who were born. Cindy stopped my story and asked, *"How did I know all of this stuff? You didn't see the whole world, did you? How did you leave Conrad and enter the minds of Maria and of Noah?" How come I never heard about this stuff? Why do you keep talking about the Pleistocene Extinction when it's not in the History books as a big deal?"*

Then she yelled out, *"You talked to Noah! I just talked to someone who talked to Noah and his wife. How is this possible?"* Then she checked her pulse to see if she was dreaming or whatever.

I could see I was losing her and I did not want her to sign me up for one of those frontal lobotomies, so I began telling Cindy scientific details about how the Pleistocene Extinction and Worldwide flood came about that had nothing to do with me so she could understand how very bad it would be for these people I was talking with and having intimate feelings about, to do some inappropriate action to mess up our time-line. Ultimately, I was "sent" to help them do what our current reality established for them to do.

I asked her if she had heard about the millions of woolly mammoths who were quickly frozen in Siberia with flowers still in their mouths at the end of the Pleistocene. She said, *"I think so!"*

I asked if she had heard of the thousand years of warring depicted by what scientists laughingly call the "Younger Dryas"? She said, *"I did hear something about a period called the Younger Dryas, but I didn't know it was the time of a massive wars."*

I asked if she heard about the ½ million craters called the "Carolina Bays" that covered the east coast of the United States and whose impacts were traced back to the end of the Pleistocene. She said, *"No!"* so I showed her the details and explained how much of the Earth caught fire as massive meteorites burrowed into the ground and set the forests aflame between 10 and 11 thousand years ago.

I then asked if she had heard about a highly advanced Island nation of Undall and its capitol called Atlantis; and how this commercial and technological hub had been ruled by the father of the first true Pharaoh of Egypt who was named Thoth? I then made a stupid comment that I was not talking with a lisp. She said, *"Who hasn't heard of Atlantis? I was told it was just a made-up story by Plato. As far as Thoth, I just happened to be reading about the gods of Egypt not long ago and Thoth's name was all over the place. The Egyptians drew him as a man with and stupid Ibis head. Don't tell me a stupid bird-head pharaoh of Egypt came from Islands that sank in the Ocean."*

I chuckled but knew this effort to suppress history was rampant in almost all classrooms, besides mine and I would have to take it slowly. I told her, the Atlantis civilization and its destruction are found in many, many ancient texts around the world, besides the great work of Plato. I then said, the great Egyptian Pharaoh, Thoth, who came from this nation, made Egypt a technological capitol as his guiding hand allowed a great machine to be built that affected the entire world. Today we find the remains of the machine, and it is still being studied today. Unfortunately, the quasi-anthropologists try to make the machine, or Great Pyramid, out to be a massive casket.

Readers: While I would not be with Thoth on this adventure. I actually, would be able to talk with him in a much different mission and at a later time under some very strange circumstances. What a neat guy.

I know I was losing her again and added, *"This stuff will make more sense as I tell you more about this "visitation" I had stumbled onto. I promise"* After allowing her to think about my questions and previous statements a little while and after I got some water she had on her table, I continued.

Maria, Lamech, Noah, and this man Conrad, who I had "invaded", would soon or had already been intimately affected by this Pleistocene season of War that would end everything they had built up. After seeing Noah, I told Conrad I would be with him again if that was ok. He said it was fine with him, so I tried to think of other things and found myself back in my own time sitting on my own couch. No! I didn't clap my shoes together and recite *"There is no place like home,"* three times like in the movies, I just was home and I don't know how that works.

I decided to do a little research on the whole Atlantis thing and the Destruction of Rahab before I went back for more confirmations and I showed Dr. Cindy what I had found from the works of King Thoth of Egypt. I had critiqued his works which have helped me in some of my time-travel events and I reviewed them to fill in background Dr. Cindy needed to believe me. If she didn't believe me, she certainly would not be able to help me.

Pleistocene Writings

I showed Cindy elements of where and how King Thoth's *"Emerald Tablets"* provided a wide assortment of truths to the people living during the Pleistocene and those following in our current Holocene Age. As far as Theological Philosophy, I suppose you could consider him to be like Plato of the Greeks or Isaiah of the Jews.

While many immediately turn to the Bible and the Sciences, I had recently read a translation of the Emerald Tablets which were first written down around 3000 BC. It's sort of a history, science, and religion set of books and I knew it would give me insights as Thoth was a strong believer of the Creator God and he wrote about many of the secrets and technologies I was seeing with my own eyes. It also provided evidence that Thoth ruled Egypt during the last part of the Pleistocene, the destruction of Venus, the sinking of Atlantis, during the Worldwide Flood, and into the Holocene Age. His works confirmed the sinking of the great technologically advanced Atlantis that was later reported by Plato, and the tablets described how time and space were related. Thoth informed us that he built his Electricity making Pyramid during the Pleistocene and informed us that people used flying machines for transport, and much more. The Pleistocene people were not backward; they were highly advanced. Some could say too advanced for their carnal minds as technology pushed the quasi-Extinction of the world.

After my discussions of this great work, Cindy was in shock and said to me, *"I thought the Egyptians were all polytheistic worshippers who were essentially backward outside of the remarkable building of massive Pyramids, and the strange writing. Now it seems they made electricity, that powered the world, flew around in aircraft and, possibly, helped develop the "Unclean/ abominable" animals that were responsible for God destroying the entire world."*

I said, *"Hold on just a little. Egypt and Thoth were not responsible for God's wrath. Let me show you a few more things before we get back to Conrad."* I pulled up another section of historical texts from the Jewish Essene to clarify why the Earth had been destroyed 10 thousand years ago. These works included segments from a number of canonized and sacred texts including: *"Adam and Eve II", "Jubilees", "Enoch", "Pesher of the Periods", "Apocalypse of Baruch", "Wisdom", "Reuben", and "Origins of the World".* I had used this group in an Ancient Human Biologic Anthropological paper I had written describing this time in the Pleistocene. This actually was from before my actual trip. I told her to just read what she wanted to, but the paper would help her understand and believe what was going on. I was really hoping she would not think I was a nutcase. She skimmed through the paper and noted various elements.

"Adam and Eve II" described "Unbridled Sex" of the Cainites and Anak during the Pleistocene.

"Origins of the World" provided details of the wars and the destruction of Venus.

"Jubilees 12" described how the Earth's axis shifted at the time of the worldwide flood which occurred 7 time-periods after Venus was destroyed.

"Pesher of the Periods" described how the Anak people had giant children and instigated the Pleistocene Wars.

"Apocalypse of Baruch" confirmed the Anak people had sex with the daughters of Cain and how that was part of the reason for the Pleistocene Extinction.

"Wisdom" confirmed the Giant offspring all died in the Pleistocene Wars and how righteous people escaped in various vehicles.

"Enoch 10" provided great detail about the Anak, their offspring, and the Wars. It also tells explains that all who trusted in the Creator God survived the Pleistocene Extinction.

"Genesis 7" told us "seven time-periods" after the destruction of Venus, the Pleistocene Extinction occurred and only people who were not on dry land [in boats or flying machines] survived the Extinction. To make sure readers understood, Moses repeated it 5 more times.

"Wow!", she said, *"Why aren't more scientists and historians telling others what life was like back then? I had no idea the Bible told about others surviving the flood besides Noah and his family."*

I told her, *"Religious zealots won't say anything as it goes against dogmatic beliefs and most historians cannot go against the hardline evolutionists for some reason. Scientist reject these details because it would go against what their fellow scientists had proclaimed.*

After this first paper, I presented another based on what I had seen and why this version of history made absolute sense. Many just could not handle the truth. Speaking of a truth, I told her as sort of a warning, *"I had better prepare you for what I will be finding out very soon during my travels through time as Venus is about to get destroyed,11 thousand years ago, not millions of years ago as some have tried to describe without any proof."*

Rahab Destruction

"I will find out this part affected Conrad and some of his family directly. I know this was too much for her, but I had to ask one more question about this critical time in man's development. I asked if she knew about the destruction of the Planet Venus just before the end of the Pleistocene?'

Just as I thought, she said, *"No way! I'm pretty sure I read Venus was destroyed millions of years ago from too much carbon dioxide in something called Greenhouse gas runaway, just like what we could be facing if we continue eating cows whose flatulence is too powerful to sustain our planet or drive cars that use gasoline."*

I was almost as sad as when I asked that same question to my students and got an almost identical answer. Besides hundreds of ancient descriptions of the destruction of Venus and physical evidence. Our historians have ignored, ignored, and ignored almost every piece of evidence just to make it look like carbon dioxide is bad for our planet in some way. While I had first-hand experience, I'm pretty sure my voice would not change the absurdity. Hopefully, I can save Cindy the misery of absurdity.

I pulled up another very short paper I had written on the destruction of Venus so what Conrad and others would tell me would make more sense to her. As she read, I commented on the significance and why others seemed to ignore these details. As I was giving her the information, I wondered if I was given a desire to learn about these events prior to my trip so I could help the people I must help. Our creator works in mysterious ways and maybe he was preparing me for my work years ahead of actually sending me on missions to "correct-time".

I told her, *"Everywhere you look, you find more and more details about Venus destruction near the end of the Pleistocene; that it was inhabited by soldiers fighting for the Anak known as Satan, and it was destroyed during one of the wars; that the destruction cause a million of more meteors to hit the Earth and set it on fire during the time called Younger Dryas; and that as Venus was in the process of destruction, a massive ribbon of fire was displayed in the sky which was seen by every living human on our planet."*

Psalms 89- indicated God destroyed the Vain planet to regain the heavens.

Isaiah 51:9-10 -indicated God destroyed the Vain planet [Rahab] which wounded Satan's Army

Job 26:12- indicated Satan's Army was destroyed when the Planet Rahab was reduced to stones of fire.

Enoch 85:1-4 indicated when Venus fell, many pieces followed.

Greek legend- indicated a blazing star set fire to Earth before it became Venus.

PreInca legend - called Venus the wavy-haired planet.

PreAztec legend - called Venus "the Star that smoked" and that it once killed many people.

Blackfoot Indian legend- said Venus put on a scarlet cloak as pieces of it returned to Earth.

Ute legend- Thousands of pieces of Venus fell to Earth causing a general fire.

Phoenician legend- Venus descended into a pool as a "fiery falling star".

Indian legend-Venus grew smaller and killed everyone in sight. <u>Her hair flew in the sky and the world trembled.</u>

Assyrian legend – Venus [Ishtar- pronounced Easter] ran down like flames and made heaven and Earth shake. Ishtar descended from the sky in an Egg [meteor].

I knew Dr. Cindy had a lot to think about and some of this might still seem too strange for truth right now, but I thought I needed to get her open to what I was going to tell her on my next "Visit", which was decided to be the following Saturday. I made a stupid comment about Ishtar Eggs hitting the Earth and she laughed. We both left and I went home.

Later that evening, I got a call from my therapist. She said, *"I had a wonderful time and the reason I got so quiet was the amount of history I had no idea about and I am truly excited to find out how you helped these people."*

I told her how very much she was helping me understand me. I also told her she did have beautiful brown eyes for a doctor.

There was a sigh! And then, *"Good Night!"*

Important Return

I'm sure my students were glad for my therapy as I really was interfacing with them better. One student brought in two arrowheads from the Sumerian times and showed them to the class along with a report about the smallness of the wars during the ancient times. While I did smile a bit, I told him that I really appreciated all the work he put in the report and had the class give him a round of applause for the details he had investigated. To tell the truth, after the Great Babel War, 55 hundred years ago, mankind did drift back into a life of backwardness, and I did not want them to misunderstand other details I had given them to expand their awareness while not getting into trouble with the faculty. Anyway, I had a great week and Saturday came again. My therapist and I met at her home and she made me Pizza. OK! She had the pizza delivered, but she put it on a plate and said where are we going back in time today?

"Wow! I guess I had better get to it.", I said. *"We are going to get Conrad out of the Army."*

The next morning after I had met the great Noah, I reinitiated my link and was with Conrad in an instant, but something was terribly wrong. I found him in his lab with an "Inspector" of some kind, selecting volunteers for the on-going battles. Conrad had already had an "encounter with this guy on a previous visit and I could tell he was extremely worried about the outcome of this "selection". I informed him I was there and for him to try to shake the "Inspectors" hand so I could see what I could do. As the guy came nearby Conrad, he turned and faced him. Conrad quickly gave the appearance that he was fainting and brushed up against this guy's arm. That was all I needed and linked to this guy, carefully trying to guide what he was saying and introducing reason for his words.

Instead of selecting Conrad as one of the volunteers, he said, *"You appear to need medical attention, please see the nurse. Your work here is too valuable for transfer at this time."* Conrad left the room immediately and discovered later that 23 of his coworkers had been reassigned to the War effort. This left only 14 engineers in the entire lab. It would be highly unlikely there would be any additional volunteer requirements.

Conrad told me it had been 2 years since my last visit and I explained I could not control this odd time variance. Conrad took the opportunity to leave work early both to morn those "selected" and to celebrate. One of those selected, Jothan, was one of his closest friends and one who was going with him during the extinction event, so he made a quick stop at his friend's house to comfort Jothan's wives.

The statistics of the wars for non-Anak soldiers was dismal as I found out with over half never returning home. He had called ahead and Jothan's wives were waiting. They knew what he was going to say and they had already received word of his volunteer status. In tears, Conrad hugged them and whether I liked it or not I felt all of their pain and suffering. I was then that Conrad told the women, Jamma and Susan, that if anything happened, he would take over husbandism if they wanted him. For whatever reason, I felt that while both welcomed this "invitation", Susan already had feelings for him, from some other encounter. This disturbed me, but later I understood more lividly than one could imagine. Conrad made his departure notification and the two women kissed him very deeply as he left for home.

Oh No!

When Conrad got home, Maria was waiting at the front door and she greeted him, and me, by default, with a kiss. I'm not talking about closed lip kiss, it was just like Susan had just given him earlier. For a moment I thought, *"This invading affectionate people was not so bad."* Conrad chuckled at what I thought was a personal thought.

They went into the house and Conrad explained all that had happened to him and what had happened to Jothan. He also explained that he had "invited" Jamma and Susan to be additional wives if something happened. Maria comforted him even more and exclaimed she was certainly glad for Susan as she had indicated she had strong feelings for Conrad. I was truly stunned, but then a knock at the door was followed by another woman entering and her name I found out was Lily and she was Conrad's wife.

As it turned out, women typically married 2 men for "varied companionship within a clan". Lily was one of the wives of a man in "city planning". His name was Arnold but Lily had decided to be with Conrad for a while and Arnold was not a believer. I also found that Maria had another husband who had died in the War already, so she could get a second husband whenever she desired, but for the past 25 years she only had Conrad.

Conrad's Clan

Conrad told me about his family. He and the others of his group were of the Inrushan clan. While one of the Inrush family held the "kingship" of Hanar at this time, they were distant cousins. Conrad's wife, Maria, was daughter to his uncle's, wife's, brother's, daughter, while Lily, was actually his 1st cousin. Jothan was not an Inrush. He was of the Nimrodian clan who had been in power before an Inrush became king. Jothan's, wife Jamma was actually his half-sister while Susan had ties to both the Nimrodians and Inrush as Jothan's grandfather had married an Inrush as an honor bride for heroism and friendship with the Inrush family, so Conrad, thought of Jothan as family as well. He was even invited to some of the "get to know you" parties that were common at that time.

Then there was another knock on the door and I was about to understand more what a "get to know you" party really was. Another good-looking woman came in named Bonnie. She reached over and hugged the other women and then gave Conrad, and me, by default, a long kiss. When her lips made contact, I knew she was the wife of Conrad's clan friend named Reese, and she was there for some sexual excitement. As the other two hugged and kissed Conrad, I knew they had similar plans.

Bonnie said to Conrad, *"Is James, that future guy, with you?"* Conrad said, *"James is with me, but he can only stay for a day at a time and we don't know when he will be back."* She came back with, *"We had better make his visit worthwhile."* The other two girls said, *"Let's make sure he comes back soon."*

I took a sip of water before I continued with the details that might be objectionable to Cindy. I looked up and asked my doctor if the details of intimate connections would help her analysis. I was pretty sure she knew what was coming, but she said the details may be very helpful. Generally knowing, from my quick connection with her, she wasn't overly embarrassed by the topic, so I proceeded, cautiously.

"Back with Conrad, my brain was spinning, but it was about to get really strange as Bonnie, Lily, and Maria took Conrad and disrobed him and took him into a large bathtub where they joined him. Lily introduced herself to me, and said, *"This is going to be fun."* Lily asked about sex in the future just like Maria had done earlier. Bonnie added, *"I'll bet we do a better job at having fun."* It wasn't long before I was certain she was correct. The "event" included ice, sweet smelling oil, and various combination I did not know were practical. I must add there was also a lot of noises. While they directed much of their efforts to insure Conrad was well satisfied after almost being drafted, my name was also proclaimed during various moments of climactic completions.

At one point I thought about how pretzels were twisted up on top of different layers, but I was having trouble thinking too much. Conrad was thinking, *"What in the world are pretzels? I think James is having a good time."* The smells of the oils and the temporary jolt of ice followed by something entirely different had Conrad and his visitor, me, almost screaming in joyous exclamation. OK! Conrad did all the male yelling.

It wasn't long before I understood what real stamina was all about and I was glad for Conrad's capabilities. In no way did what I had experienced seem like the exercises of a group of 4 people over 4-hundred Jubilee years old, trying to show off to a guy sitting inside one of their heads. Then Bonnie came closer to Conrad and whispered, *"James! You should see what it's like when we get a group of 10 in an Inrush Clansman bedroom."*

I could see Dr. Cindy was losing the Dr. identity, so I greatly abbreviated the all-night session except for one important part; *"Each time one of the women touched Conrad, I felt all the intensity of both Conrad and their multiple and varied interfaces. I was thinking, "Pleistocene humans not only had stamina, but they felt intense love for each other." Oddly, I sensed that each of my four Pleistocene companions had the idea that my presence had increased their stamina and compassion immensely. It was not long before I realized, my "invasion" had energized each of them and had increased their compassion for each other. I had a theory about why.*

I stopped my description for a moment to explain to my Doctor, what I believed had caused the capability of a 4-hour sexual exercise. *"It is my belief, and I have an incredible perspective about this matter, that our soul regulates how we interface in what we call reality. When 2 souls are interacting in a single "self", we sense "reality" twice as intently. Think of it like a battery that "turns on" a computer. If two batteries are used to power the computer, it can stay on twice as long or it can suck out twice as much electricity during its operation. Two souls intensify and extend our interface with reality. What we see gets more contrast, our bodies have more stamina, and our feelings are more intensified. Later, I would find out this was not the only thing my "intrusion" could accomplish."*

"Besides this strange effect, the "good and bad" part of my "gift" is that I feel the same love, hate, anger, and elation of those I am with. I could not claim I did not have strong feelings for these people and others that I have "touched" and that is the main reason I am very standoffish about my students, colleagues, and everyone else as there is a lot of hate, bitterness, fear, jealousy, and hurt feelings. That is why I wear gloves everywhere I go. It usually is too confusing, frustrating, and painful. Over the years, I have figured out how to separate from my hosts in a less traumatic way, but this first time would cause me to go into a horrible time of self-loathing, abandonment, fear, hatred, and great sadness.

Cindy could certainly tell these feelings had returned from the reenactment of the previous encounter and she quietly held my gloved hand and said, *"We are going to make you better, I promise. Your gift seems to be much more a blessing than curse and I am certain, you saved Conrad's life and encouraged Noah just by being there."* I put my head on her lap and began crying like a baby. No---I mean I had a few tears. None of that baby stuff.

After my stupid outburst I got up thanked her immensely and went to leave. I turned and asked if we could continue next week and I made an appointment. She kissed me on the cheek and somehow my great sadness subsided as I left because I felt her soul. She really cared that I would somehow understand and not fear my gift. There were other feelings as well, but I knew I needed to stay separate from her as a woman.

I said, *"Good night doc,"* and I left.

Venus Destruction

I arrived on time to my "session" after letting my class out and I again sat in what I considered "My Chair". Dr. Cindy sat across from me and after saying Hi! And all the usual stuff, Dr. Cindy briefly reviewed the last part of my description, as if I would have forgotten, and I was going to continue my story, but as I looked around, there was a large picture of a man hanging by one hand from a rock that looked like it was half a mile in the air. As I looked closer, the man had one ear higher than the other. Stupidly, I asked if that was her old boyfriend. She turned around and said, *"Yes! He was a champion rock climber."*

I looked down at my body and wondered if I could climb a low hill, much less having muscles needed for something like that. I shrugged it off and said, *"Let me continue."*

"It would be about a week before I returned back in time to the Pleistocene. I could not believe what could happen in such a short time, but then I found out it had been an additional 2 years since my last visit. Conrad filled me in on some very strange news. Both Maria and Bonnie had gotten pregnant during our "exchange". Bonnie had a baby boy, she named, Tyler, and Maria had a baby girl named Becka. Conrad was so proud as having babies had not been an easy thing to do. I found out that most women quit having children after having one baby as the government instructed each to take a "birth control" substance. Conrad's "boy" and Reese's "girl" had been in the many wars

and both had died in battle. That had been over 8 hundred years ago and very few children were ever born after the birth control elixir had been taken. There were thoughts that something had been put in the drinking water that reduced childbirth rates. For whatever reasoning, it was not a common thing to have a baby.

The evidence suggested that when my soul linked up with each of the women, whatever had limited their conception had been "reestablished". Conrad told me that Lily was certain I had something to do with the babies and had she claimed another night alone with Conrad on my return. I tried not to think about that as things were getting crazy during this return visit.

Just like I had told Conrad would happen, the war had escalated to the Anak outpost on Venus. While to anyone reading the Bible and dozens of other ancient descriptions, it is fairly common knowledge today of the colonization of the planet Rahab [Vain Place] and how it was turned into an uninhabitable wasteland including turning a portion of the planet, or it's moon, into a massive number of "stones-of-fire or meteors" that struck the Earth and set it ablaze not long before the end of the Pleistocene. The destruction of Venus had not happened yet.

Cindy stopped me and said, *"Now I see why you filled me up with all that Planet Rahab stuff last time."*

While there were other colonists on the beautiful planet Venus at this time, there also was a garrison of Army troops who somehow reported to the most famous Anak named Satan.

After a brief interlude, I continued. *"Conrad told me he had heard of an Army battalion on our closest planetary neighbor and the News had told everyone that the outpost had been destroyed. Looking in the sky showed what appeared to be a massive comet with a tail that seemed to almost reach the Earth, but Conrad went on. On news descriptions, the reporters indicated something had happened on Venus, but they were* holding the details as they might affect the ongoing and continuous wars.

Conrad told me he had even visited the place about 25 years ago. As it turned out he brought his newly devastated wife, Maria, with him on his business trip. [I recalled her other husband, Sam, had lost his life in the endless wars.]

"The place was beautiful except for places where war had destroyed various outposts." he told me. Then Conrad went over to a pile of notebooks and pulled out a red one. From inside, He showed me holographic images of his trip and the cities, massive waterways and beautiful mountains. Most of what he showed me is still visible today, except the water disappeared, the pressure shot way up and the temperature turned into that of an inferno in a matter of weeks after some catastrophe. Conrad didn't know what happened and the State controlled news never said anything. Conrad went outside again and in the daytime one could see the planet's tail almost reaching the Earth.

I stopped and showed Cindy a tiny portion of the evidence collected concerning inhabitation of our "twin" planet. Here are some of the things we find on Rahab, I mean Venus, today. The pressure and heat there are way too high to support life now, but it can easily be seen the planet used to be filled with beauty and populations of colonists.

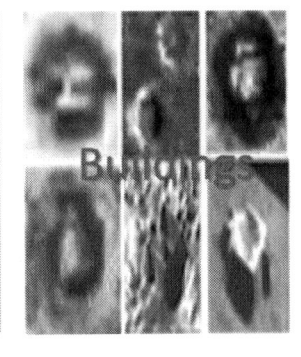

I would find out later what Conrad was seeing was a plasma tail showing the vastly different Earth and Venus electrical potentials had almost been high enough to cause a massive electrical discharge. A common belief is the moon came between the two planets at just the wrong time and it filled in the Plasma separation. As the Venusian moon came between the two planets scientists believe, it burst into millions of pieces and destroyed the entire planet in a matter of a few hours. Right now, I wanted to prepare Conrad and his strange collection of wives, and such, for the events that would affect them very soon.

I told him, *"In a very short time, a massive bombardment of meteors would hit the coastline of the Western continent and it would essentially catch fire. The bombardment would also shake the Earth and Earthquakes would be felt as ocean tides and levels would rise quickly to destroy the commercially significant Islands of Atlantis. As all this happened, the Earth would go into a massive time of famine. I could tell he was afraid as were the others in the room as Conrad relayed everything that he got from me in unspoken words.*

Worldwide Destruction 7-Time-periods Later

After he got his head around the first onslaught, I continued, *"The famine would signal the 7 time-periods described in the Book of Genesis between the reduction in the intensity of the war and the final shifting of the Earth that would cause massive changes in weather, would cause the polar Ice Caps to melt and refreeze causing worldwide floods, followed by and massive destruction by mile high tidal waves around the globe. No-one on land will survive it; no animals and no people."*

As anyone would have, Conrad felt even more fear for his family and, of course, Conrad asked, *"How long was 7-time periods.* "I told him, *"Noah would know as he, evidently, told people about the timing."* Conrad indicated he would visit Noah and hope it would help him prepare. As before, Conrad's resolve and bravery concerning this horror, was probably aided by my interface.

My heart went out to all hearing what I was saying, *"I can say is it will be long enough for substantial misery from famine caused by the disruption and onslaught of the Earth. My suggestion is, to get as much food and stores as possible, find protection as the war will certainly come closer to home than it is today, and many will try to take any food you have during the hardships of this "7-time periods". Then, you must prepare some type of vehicle that can do 2 things.*

It must be able to not be destroyed during a 40-day onslaught and unthinkable tidal waves, and two; it must allow you to live inside for at least 4 or 5 months. Once you do find a suitable place to land, you would be wise to bring articles needed to sustain your life for a while on land. You will need seeds and farming equipment, books and, information about how to rebuild." Also insure you bring people who will help you rebuild humanity."

"I could feel the fear in Conrad was subsiding, but I could also see fear on the faces of the others as they watched on their viewers some of the details of the destruction of Venus as it unfolded and listened as I spoke through Conrad. Conrad also touched each of those present so that I was able to provide them with more resolve and hope. This reduced their fear as best I could. As far as any of Conrad's close family knew, none of their loved ones was on the doomed planet and Conrad jumped up and said, *"I have the vehicle under control."* It seems he, and two close clansmen, Reece and Bartlet had found an abandoned airship in the high desert. Conrad said something about how glad he was that someone had to leave their spaceship so long ago so that his family would have a way out. While there was no telling how long the ship had been abandoned, but it was at least a hundred years old and the desert had kept it almost in a *"working" state. The three of them had been working on the ship for about 2 years to make it flight worthy. Bonnie, Reece's wife, and Maria also helped whenever they could.*

Conrad indicated it was an "M45 class", originally suitable for space travel and it was similar to the one he had been in during his Venus trip. It, possibly would never be able to move away from Earth's orbit again, but they had gotten it off the ground about 6 months prior and gotten it into orbit and the team was steadily making the accommodations better and better so that it could, eventually, become a clan getaway craft for vacations. Once the gravitational-field-elimination-devices became standard elements in aircraft hundreds of years ago, it became efficient to make long trips to remote regions of the Earth. In fact, going into orbit until the earth brought your destination to you was the easiest way to travel. This type of engine would also allow for a 6-month voyage to be accomplished without having to go to a filling station. Now it appeared this would be what they needed to escape the end of the world. Both Reece and Bartlet were practically geniuses when it came to flying machines and their internal machinery. Additionally, Bartlet was an excellent and experienced pilot.

We drove out to remote site and he showed me what appeared to be a large spaceship. It had 3 orbs on the base and portholes all around the hemispherical bubble in the center. The ship was large enough for at least 14 people and room for sleeping and for a substantial amount of food and articles I had suggested. Currently, there were 10 people had signed up to something that would end up being an <u>act of treason</u> as soon as there was no reasonable time left for waiting.

"Conrad had a sack full of stores he took up to the vessel and I saw one of his friends, named Bartlet, who had been taking his turn guarding the vehicle. Conrad shook his hand and I immediately knew he had lost two close family members to the war and that he had a son who did not believe in the extinction prophesy. He knew he would probably have to leave his son or risk capture whenever the risky departure had to take place. His son's name was Shepard and he was the supervising agent for supplies for the war effort in one of the sectors of the city. To make this tragedy worse, his second wife, Shepard's mom, possibly would not go either, as she could never leave her son.

I comforted him as best I could and told Conrad I would return as soon as I could to see if there was anything I could do. Then I told him, his finding that ship must have been an act of God showing them they would be saved. That's when I ran into Lily. She took Conrad into a separate room and had her way with him "several times". She was not about to miss out on motherhood.

Just before I "left", as Conrad was getting tired, the sky turned red as what seemed like a red flashlight shined from the planet Venus to near the ground. I know this was the beginning of the end. It was just as the ancients had described. It looked like the planet Venus had a fiery tail, but I knew it was already completely destroyed. While the Bible is simply filled with descriptions of God eliminating the planet and those waging war from the planet. Today, we believe it was a natural phenomenon, however, all nature is driven by God, so God would be associated with the end of Venus. Both Maria and Bonnie brought their children over to Conrad so I could sit with them a while. Conrad picked each one up and I spoke to their souls and told them to do whatever their parents told them. After a quick kiss of the little ones and a quick cheek kiss from Maria, I thought about home and soon I was back.

Back home I took a shower and made me a sandwich. Then, as I had been doing, I wrote down significant elements to help me remember as much as possible. Within a short time, I went to bed but I dreamed about disaster after disaster. I was glad for the sun to rise.

To Conrad Again

I made sure, my body was fed properly, I laid down, and as fast as I could, I reasserted the link between me and Conrad. I had to do whatever I could to help these people; besides, I told myself, I may really have had something to do with the children who would be saved.

I could see Cindy had been trying not to cry. She hugged me and I felt her compassion for these people and empathy for me. Wiping her eyes, Cindy said, *"If you are up for it, can we continue tomorrow? I just have to know what happened to these people you were living here thousands of years before I was born."*

Atlantis

The next day would be Sunday, but I told her I would be their early in the morning if she wanted me there.

The very next day we met in a small coffee shop near my home. I told her this was going to be a fast-paced story today and everything became unglued all at one time. This next visit had Venus setting the earth on fire, massive flooding and a foolhardy attempt at rescue.

I began my story again.

"Conrad was almost in a state of terror when I reached him as Earthquakes had erupted and there was news of massive flooding. While in my normal time, it had only been hours, it had been about a year since the fiery tail of Venus marked destruction and I had last visited. Conrad was hoping the flooding was not the final signal for the end of the world. They simply were not ready. I quickly calmed him down but I also told him to increase his vigilance and many may think this is the end. With their fear, they may begin destroying as much as they could and riots probably would occur. He told me that every day since I had left, there had been acts of terror and vandalism. He told me he came home along a different route each day to help protect his family. I had to quickly ease his concerns.

I asked if the names Atlantis, Undall, or Thoth meant anything to him. He told me he had been to Undall. Conrad said. *"The Islands were the main commercial hub between the Eastern Continent and the Western one [Americas]."*

He continued, *"I made three different deliveries of animals there. The last one was about 15 years ago for my company and I remember that the High Priest's name was Thotme. He was one of the Anak who ruled the place, but he seemed different than many of the self-absorbed rulers of many places. The capitol, that I called Atlantis, was a beautiful place and a massive airport continued to have aircraft go between continents every single day, even during the war."*

I told him Thotme was Thoth's father according to ancient texts. Conrad said he loved the Kingdom of Hanar better than the hustle and bustle of Undall, especially since there are very few Anak people in their community." He made a reference about the Kingdoms of Enoch and Palai having more of the giants than you could count. He made a comment about how evil those kingdoms were as they also had many of the people known a Mystifiers in both kingdoms. While they were similar to the people of Hanar, their use of incantations and magic and the fact that the Palai people had destroyed the original capitol of Hanar and their beautiful palace about 700 years earlier showed they would not be saved from this destruction.

Conrad told me more of the news about fires around the world, the meteors, and earthquakes. For certain, Venus had been destroyed; the meteors had fallen; fires had been set; and volcanoes had caused a great swelling of the ocean waters. His concerns about the flooding was making him shake, but the Kingdom of Hanar was far from the Seas. I told him many people would not be affected by this first time of flooding.

I told him I read about the details in a number of texts. They all said the same thing. King Thoth and 33 other Anak humans escaped the sinking of Atlantis and Undall. They went to Egypt to continue what Thoth had started with his electric generator, Pyramid and to train the people of Egypt. The texts indicate that he and his companions saw their home sink into the Ocean while leaving in a flying ship. I also told him, the sinking of Atlantis and Undall was probably happening as we spoke and that was the cause of the earthquakes and flooding. I then asked if he visited Noah to find how much time he had before the flood.

Noah's Insight

Conrad said, *"I visited Noah again and he asked about you and he wanted to thank you again for encouraging him. Noah told me that from the time Rahab was destroyed until the flood was not exactly known, but he believed it would be about 2 solar years from the destruction of Rabab which was about a year ago."* He also indicated they were very close to filling their ship that he now called his "Flying Ark" after the name Noah had called his floating Ark. Not only had Conrad filled the ship with all types of food and supplies, but he also brought on board a wide assortment of DNA strands that could be used to re establish all types of animals that might not have been practical for Noah. One animal was a very large plant eating dinosaur that I would find out later was captured by the Sumerians and the Egyptians who made them pets. He certainly had sheep, goats, cows, chickens, and even the Ostrich that he had invented. Several animals were corralled to take on board directly as well.

Conrad suddenly became sad and said, *"Both Lamech and his father Methuselah were killed in a raid on the plateau. The people were after the Ark, but a massive hailstorm struck the fighters and forced them down the side of the mountain. Many of the intruders were killed in the attack, but almost none of those who were left in Shulon with Noah and his children. There were only 6 other men and 6 women left, but they swore to Noah to fight off those who would come in the last days. Knowing they would soon be killed, those on the mountaintop were extremely sullen even with what many described as an angel from God had been near them and had promised to stand with them in the last days. The leader of this faithful group was named Banyon, He* was Noah's brother. I was amazed at how resolved this group was to ensure the safety of the 'Chosen Ones' during the last hours."

Then Conrad said. *"I told Banyon that if we could we would try to pick up any survivors on the plateau before destruction,"* but Banyon said, "You must not as we have been told by an angel of God, he would take care of us."

Change Topics to Jothan

I asked if he had heard anything from Jothan and the war? Conrad said, *"Jothan had been shot in the arm and was in a holding area for repair awaiting shipment back to the war front."* He continued by telling me Jothan's wives were beside themselves with worry. They had been allowed to visit once and he told them he would be repaired in the next few days as the projectile that had struck him was a small caliber bullet and part of his arm was still intact.

Dr. Cindy stopped me and said, *I thought you said they had nuclear weapons and missiles and all the rest, are you pulling my leg about the -bullet?"*

I told her massive weapons were in use according to a number of accounts including something described as a "Sword of Light" in sacred book *"Generations of Adam"*. Possibly, they called it that because they had not seen a Star Wars movie and did not know the proper terminology was "Light Sabre", but the main thing is, there were hundreds of types of weapons. The weaponry included their version of rifles. The effects of high speed small projectile weapons are fairly common in Pleistocene human and animal remains.

Cindy said, *"Ok, Ok!" I knew it was going to be something about our history books coving up facts. I'm so glad you came to me to tell this story, you have no idea how very much you are helping me with my own set of demons and when I say demons I know what I'm talking about."*

I wasn't sure what she was talking about when she mentioned demons, but, as always, I took out my trusty computer and showed her a horrible image of many humans and even some animals that had evidently died by gunshot during the Pleistocene. While the majority were Cro-Magnon hybrids, some were Neanderthal and one was a long headed Anak hybrid. These human remains have been found around the world in Russia, Middle East, Africa, South and Central America.

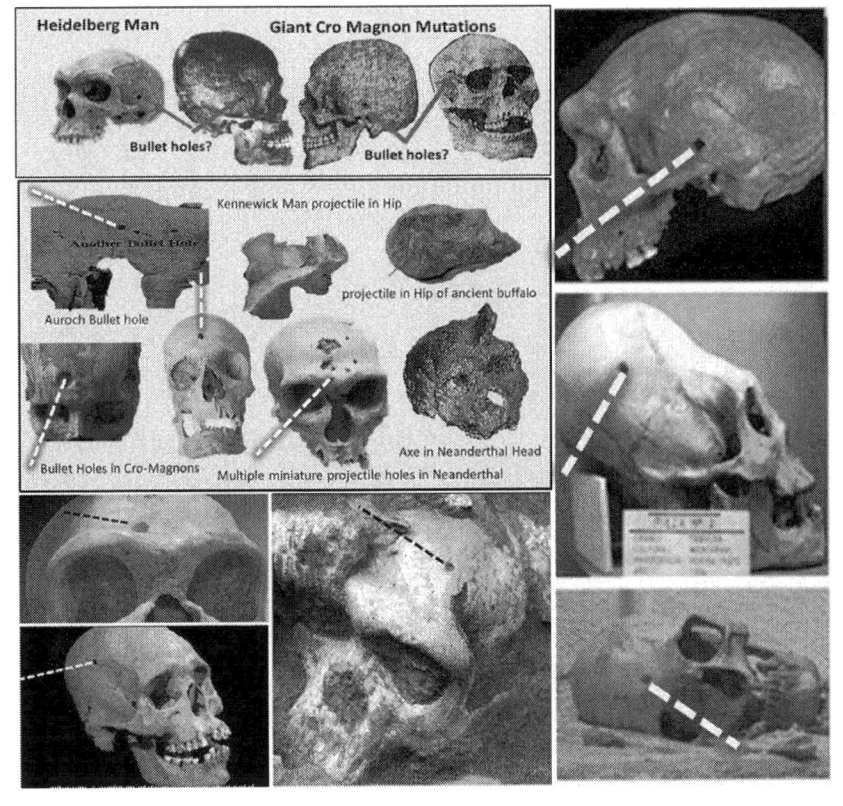

I told her, *"The reason most of the recovered evidence of high speed projectile destruction is on the skull was that 90 percent of bullets do no hit bones and the skull is a large bone. Many times,*

108

the opposite side of the entry point is much larger just like our modern rifles cause."

I told her that Conrad told me, *"The people of Palai were called Mystifiers as they channeled the mysteries of magic. The Mystifiers had destroyed the main city of Hanar and he hated the people from Palai. I had read about the weapon used. It was the Light Saber. Later I would find out this weapon was still around. I then pulled out a copy of the "Generations of Adam" and told Cindy, "This book was so sacred, they have found many copies in the Essene libraries stored in the Qumran caves in Israel. John-the-Baptist used these books when preaching to his followers. The book described force fields, missiles, and destruction of an entire town with a single blast as well as the first use of light-sabers."*

"Generations of Adam"-*Armies devastated the land. For two years, the people suffered under great desolations, as one army, then another gained dominion over various parts of the land. At the end of two years, there was destruction everywhere, and the people began to flee into the wilderness to escape the wrath which had fallen upon them, until only a small number remained with King Canaan in the ruins of the City of Haner. And the only city which remained was the City of Palai, -- a mighty noise from heaven shook the air. Whence the palace stood there was only dust. -- great barriers of power were established around the city of Haner, so that <u>no missile could penetrate</u> the forces which surrounded the city-- Leboa the daughter of Tamar, devised **a <u>sword of light</u>** which penetrated the wall of defense around the city of Haner and began to drain the power from the wall-- from their hands flashed streams of fire. And where the wall surrounding their city had almost disappeared, another wall arose in its place,*

Cindy said, *"Let's get into a different subject!"*

A told her, *"I really wasn't with Conrad long before I felt almost sick to my stomach if I had one. I was worried about leaving my body and **I felt so odd**, I simply had to leave Conrad."* Before I left, I let him know I would be back as fast as I could.

"Anyway; when I returned to my own home, I had my own issues," I told my still skeptical listener. She was going to have an even more difficult time with what I needed to tell her next.

Please do not do this EVER! It can and probably will backfire.

Not a Demon!

Everybody has heard about demons and the Bible is full of incidents with demons being forcibly removed from a person, but what do you know about demons?", I asked my understanding Doctor, who was looking at me strangely. Then she made a sign of a cross and backed away from me.

Cindy said, *"If you mean some evil satanic being that consumes a person; I don't think I really believe in them. Maybe during the Bible days, they existed, but all that exorcist stuff is only in the movies. -- Right?"*

I looked up at her and as seriously as I could I said, *"Wrong!"*

"Demons are horribly real", I quickly blurted out. *Some are very, very powerful and all can be deadly. From many different texts, we are told that there was this massive war in Heaven and 1/3 of all the inhabitants of Heaven were kicked out and changed to Anak humans. Anak simply means "giant with a long neck or head". Anyway, let's say there were at least a couple million of these people who lived for thousands and thousands of years if they weren't killed in War or some similar action that would shorten their lives. Unlike us, Anak humans had no spirits so they could never leave here to go back to heaven after death. Their souls stayed in something we could call "Limbo". The only way they could experience life again was inside a live person or animal. Most of the Anak humans would be sent to a place of torture during the last days, but some have tried their best to worship the creator over these thousands of years with*

the hope that they will be free from that eventual fate. With millions of demons around, we can believe, many people, today, are possessed. All demons are desperate to experience carnality so those people who are possessed experience, great hate, pride, sexual desire, and all types of evil. I would suggest many leaders of countries become possessed because of their overly sensitive pride.

Let me give you an example. A friend of mine name Richard Cline, decided to learn how to do that Astral Projection stuff. He got quite good and was able to feel himself float away from his body, but one day, as he was returning, he told me he knew he was not alone and, as far as I know, he never was the same again. Here I was leaving my body OFTEN.

"Why are you telling me all this?", she asked and was afraid of my answer.

I began by saying, *"When I got back to the 21st century, my body was being used!*

"Oh No!", She blurted out. *"How did you recover?"*

Remember I told you that a few Anak still held on to the belief that someday, they would be released from the chains of their rebellion and they could once again return to Heaven, well, we are told in the "Book of Ruben" that about 10 percent of the Anak were saved from death by the flood to help mankind with development of medicines, etc. Other texts tell us that only the "Righteous" were saved. My belief is the 10% identified were "good" demons. No matter! I had been possessed by an Anak demon named Jack. On my return, our souls came together just like the ones I have been telling you about. I felt the great sadness and fear of Jack and he possibly would have known about what I had been doing. After a very short and very uncomfortable time, Jack made me know that he would leave me *alone and go back to limbo, but he just had to get a tiny glimpse of reality and my body didn't seem to mind.*

Dealing with a Demon

That is when I had an idea. I made him a deal that if I leave my body he could return and use my body provided that he ensures I sleep and eat as needed and he keeps other less friendly demons from attaching themselves to me. He quickly agreed and asked what we were going to eat. I asked what he liked and he said EVERYHING. I/we had a little bit of everything and I was about to make sure he left when I had a dangerous idea.

I knew that some descriptions of demonic possessions were different than the massive evil, rage, foaming at the mouth, falling down, and general ugliness usually associated with complete loss of control of oneself. While other times, still ugly, some events were associated with super strength, climbing walls, and even flying. I asked Jack about how some possessions were described with expansion in human capabilities. He told me that on occasion, a human host and demon work in concert to a degree. While the host tries to hold onto normality, the demon barely attaches to augment reality of the host. I reasoned it as follows:

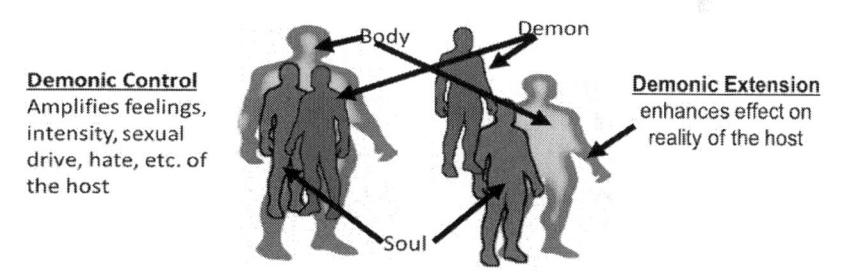

Demonic Control
Amplifies feelings, intensity, sexual drive, hate, etc. of the host

Body
Demon
Soul

Demonic Extension
enhances effect on reality of the host

If a demon could do it, possibly I could as well and with Jack being able to eat and sleep for me, I could extend my visits [in theory!]

Cindy jumped up and blurted out, *"Please tell me you did not make a deal with a demon. Are you crazy?"*

I said, *"That's why I'm seeing you.*

--- I know it's crazy, but I just had to help these people and I could not do it with afternoon outings separated by years.

Cindy, looked at me seriously and almost yelled at me, *"You are still flirting with disaster and this demon thing still------- Just quit it right now. If you can't save these people, they probably weren't supposed to be saved. Quit it -quit it -quit it!",* then she began to cry and appeared to be wondering when I would start climbing the walls and speaking in Latin and foaming at the mouth.

She was visibly shaken and scared for me. If I had heard what I told her, I might have reacted the same way. I said, *"What I'm telling you was all in the past. Let me continue."*

I hugged her for support and she got embarrassed. She wiped her tears, apologized, sat down and I continued.

"After some simple instruction from my new quasi-friend and setting up my departure with the "very nice" Jack, I grabbed the stone purse and was with Conrad in an instant.

Conrad went over to a mirror. Looking in a mirror made him more at ease to talk to me and he blurted out *"I have to get Jothan out of the hospital before they take him back. I've been planning and preparing for a "rescue" ever sense you left last time 4 months ago. While I've planned for you not being here, this will make things so much less dangerous."*

Jamma and Susan are almost dying inside when they saw Jothan a second time. I was hoping Conrad had, at least, the beginnings of a plan, and I was pretty sure I would be ok no matter what and I really felt a need to help Jothan and his wives. While Lily and Susan could not come, Maria and Jamma were ready and waiting. We were off to the military hospital within an hour or so and my head was spinning because I had a good idea what he was going to do as I was in his head.

Conrad's Rescue

From my connection with him, I understood his plan. Jamma, Jothan's wife, would ask to see him once more before he was being shipped off. This is, typically, conjugal. As was the custom, having others aid in those visits was also common. This would allow us to be separated from the rest of the facility, but we only had this one chance. That is where Conrad's biological capabilities came in. He had made a somewhat toxic, non-lethal, and fast infiltrating organism that caused great stomach pain and loss of bowel control.

As we entered, we would slowly deposit the critters along the halls and anywhere they took us. This would ensure the way back out of the facility would be open as we tried to leave. Conrad didn't have specific requirements for me but believed I could aid in some way as they tried to escape. Oh! Yes! Conrad made an antitoxin for our "team" so that we could still walk. To make the plan work, locator transmitters were removed from the three "new criminals". The plan involved leaving as fast as possible and hiding in the newly supplied aircraft until the final doom.

We reached the military hospital when it was still morning and checked in to see Jothan. He had been cleared to depart and was going through indoctrination prior to reentry into the warfront. He had lost half of his left arm and a new one was being made. He was informed he would not get the new appendage until he was safely back in the war.

We had the right paperwork and entered without issue. As we entered, we dropped infectious droplets from tubes affixed to our legs. Past the guards we entered the hospital and to the room where Jothan was to meet us, but he had not arrived yet.

While our nerves were tense, including mine, Jothan soon entered the room, but one of the guards was sent in to ensure correct actions. Conrad knew this would probably happen and we went over and touched him on the arm. I convinced him he was already sick, which was not a real stretch, and that there would be no reason to watch the unfolding of a normal encounter. He left without incident and Jamma quickly provided Jothan with the antidote. Conrad had been wearing two sets of clothes and quickly removed one set for Jothan. Conrad gave Jothan a note, generally telling him the plan. Then he made a moaning sound to add to those already in play. While Jothan was getting dressed, the women made sounds of lovemaking as the sounds from these rooms were always recorded.

Another Friend

Jothan got sick, but he could still walk. Strangely, a second guard started to enter the "visitation room" and he had not gotten sick yet. Conrad was about to grab his arm so that I could convince him to leave but Jothan stopped him and said, *"Martin is a friend."*

Conrad said, *"He's a Kite! How can he be a friend?"* It seems the people of Palai or Mystifiers had a darker complexion while most of the people of Hanar had reddish complexion. I don't know where the reference to Kites came from, but I knew it was a common name.

Jothan came back and said, *"Trust me. I wouldn't be alive if it wasn't for him. He is a believer!"*

Conrad still touched Martin's shoulder so that I could test his true feelings. What I found was extremely sad, as Martin had lost most of his family. They were some of very few believers and the Pleistocene Kingdom in the lineage of the Mystifiers who practiced all types of Necromancy. The poor man I had invaded believed in Noah's prediction and had abandoned the ways of his fathers. He had believed there was nothing he could do, but he was trying to make amends for the Mystifiers' evils by helping Jothan.

Martin proclaimed to the group he was a friend and had to get something. Within a flash he was gone.

Panic ensued and Jothan and I tried to calm everyone down. Jothan said, *"Martin will not tell anyone, I trust him with my life."*

As quickly as he left, he returned and said, *"I don't know what you guys did, but looks like everyone is sick including me."* Under his coat was the Prosthetic that was to be provided in the morning. By this time, Martin could barely stand up from stomach cramps.

I had also understood that Martin seemed to be trusting in Jothan for help if it was possible but understood there was little likelihood of his being saved from the Flood. I also knew he had one wife left, Tani, and a son named Ben. When I knew this information, I made sure Conrad knew it.

Conrad stopped and got Jamma to quickly give him the antidote. As we left the room, we acted like we were all sick and holding our stomachs. We followed Martin's lead to evade cameras and finally, we were outside well before an alarm was sounded. We got in the vehicle without incident and hid Jothan and Marin under the floorboard.

At the check-point, word of the outbreak had raised suspicion. Conrad got out of the vehicle and began discussing how sick he was feeling while he began depositing the infectious bacteria he had made and pretended to fall, holding the guard to help support him.

I suggested to the guard, "W*e were not the ones he needed to search as he had seen another suspicious person going around the corner of the hospital towards the back.*" Of course, it was all a lie, but his mind accepted the suggestion and he called for men to go around the back of the hospital as he waved us through so he could concentrate on those who had infected the hospital.

We did as he asked and left quickly. As we left, Jamma cut-out "trackers" in the arms of Jothan and Martin, which we left in a hole alongside the road to make it harder to find a location. After the minor surgery, we went overland. In the air we flew as low to the ground as safety permitted and possibly lower as a couple of treetops were nicked along the way. By now, our vehicle, along with the escaped "Army volunteers", were being tracked down. We were all fugitives, especially Martin, who helped us.

The radar type system used during this time was not substantially different that we have today and it was augmented with a tracker that used magnetic distortions for showing movement. One of those who had planned to leave with Conrad was a magnetic field engineer and he built a number of drones that appeared to have the same magnetic signature as our vehicle. All three of the drones were sent out in different directions as we went and they had been made to stay low and continue until their cinnabar plasma generator had run out of fuel. Once it was empty, it was to blow itself up to further challenge any pursuers and keep the manufacturer anonymous. Conrad's vehicle had a specific magnetic signature so Reece, designed a magnetic shadow that would characterize the vehicle as one of the smaller models not assigned to any of the wayward crew looking for safety in the upcoming catastrophe.

Here we all were 4 people from Hanar, one "Mystifier" from Palai, and my soul from the future, but I think I need to explain something about the Mystifiers.

Invisibility

I took a breather from the main story and said to my cute doctor, *"Let me back up and fill in information about the Mystifier people and how they were associated with Martin."*

"The Mystifiers were unusual, in that, they had an ability called necromancy. This did not only mean they could transmute minerals and perform stage magic. Of the various talents of the Mystifiers, the one that was to be of most importance was their ability to change the vibrational pattern of their bodies. It seems they could make a mirror image of their cells. By having both positive and negative vibrating cells, this action could make them invisible."

To describe what I meant to my doctor, I explained how noise cancelling headphones take sounds and make a mirror copy of the sound; *"When both sounds are heard together, there is "no sound" as one cancels the other. Mystifiers could do this with their body, and not only disappear, they could walk through walls during this modification, but there was a problem. When they were invisible, they could not see anything or feel anything. I told her about some of the experiments in invisibility of the Canadian researcher named John Hutchison who, in the 1990s, was able to make things vanish by irradiating them with ultra-high frequency electro-magnetic waves that cancelled out the "normal" vibrations of materials."* This "Hutchison Effect" also made materials completely weightless which allowed them to levitate.

I took out my computer to show Cindy a sampling of modern invisibility capability so I thought I would show you as well. The first 2 images show common metal object becoming completely invisible while the second set show both wood and a metal knife that became invisible and was passing through a hunk of aluminum. When the energy was turned off, the knife and a piece of wood became solid again inside the metal.

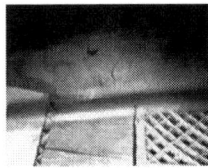

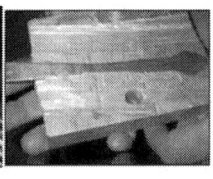

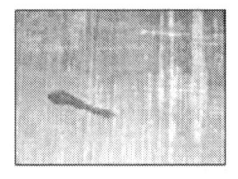

Then he made a pair of pliers and a bowling ball fly up in the air and a piece of metal changed its consistency and began to melt without heat.

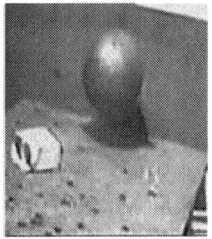

After trying to explain how scientists were making things invisible I could tell, Dr. Cindy had no idea we were actually accomplishing such things. I didn't even go into how scientists were now disintegrating subatomic particles and having them appear miles away, in an instant in an effort to understand how time goes to zero at the speed of light and space has no meaning without time. Mystifiers could do these things by actions of their minds and some slight difference in their DNA, I suppose. By mirroring the electromagnetic composition of their own bodies, they could do the same thing that Gravitons do.

To help Cindy, in case she had not studied gravitons, I explained they were particles that produced gravity, but had no "effective" mass. They were invisible just like Mystifiers could become. Mystifiers simply made their bodies seem to be gravitonic, to put it in the MODERN scientific language. I showed her a general diagram of how opposite vibrating particles make the invisibility referred to as gravitons. While one would think a graviton would weigh the same as two particles, it has absolutely no weight or shape. While it has gravity, it doesn't exist with any other characteristic.

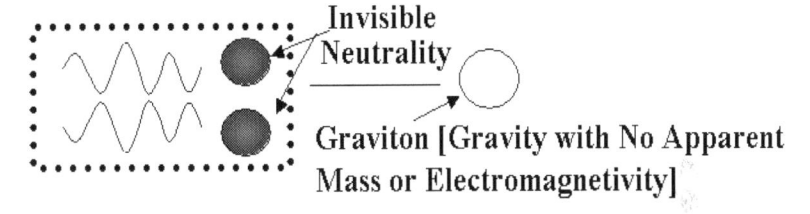

Invisible Neutrality

Graviton [Gravity with No Apparent Mass or Electromagnetivity]

With that overview, let me get back to the story and the people from the kingdom of Palai as their will be invisibility and much more.

Mystifiers

During the early years of the warring, the kingdom of Palai had attacked the people of Hanar. All this was described in the Jewish *"Generations of Adam"* book. Luckily for me, I got firsthand information from Conrad. After one attack a field of energy was erected around the main city where the King's Palace was. This shield protected the people and the Mystifiers could not go through it even when they became invisible. This is where the Mystifier woman named Leboa, [3-great granddaughter to Adam], came into the picture. The ancient book Moses referenced in Genesis 5, *"Generation of Adam"*, indicates she used a "sword of light" to suck out the energy holding the barrier to the city.

Once the barrier was down, the city was lost and Leboa became an instant hero in the Kingdom of Palai. As far as Conrad remembered, he lost one of his grandfathers, and an Aunt in that battle and many of his kinsmen in their clan were killed or wounded as the Mystifiers leveled the city and those who could escape, ran. Some of the people of Hanar were still enslaved by Palai-ites up until very recently, so Conrad, truly hated all of them. He was struggling with Martin. Now he was going to have to change his mind quickly.

Martin was crying in the back of the vehicle as he knew his family would be tortured and even killed to find the traitor he had become.

Jothan exclaimed to the others, as he was trying out his new arm, "*We have to try to get Martin's wife, Tani, and his son, Ben.*" As he said it he knew he should not have brought it up as it would place all in jeopardy, but Martin had made his life bearable in the "hospital" and he had become close to Martin's family during visitation. Even Conrad agreed, so the course was changed. At first, Conrad thought that I would not be able to help them because of my one-day requirement, but I began filling him in on my new acquaintance, Jack, the possibilities that may or may not be possible if we extended my soul, and this wild idea that I could be used to "see" for Martin when he was invisible. By nightfall, we arrived in the City of Palai where Martin lived with a wonderful plan. OK! It was a good plan. Actually, it was just a bunch of what-ifs. To get ready, Conrad and Martin, and my soul, attempted a wide assortment of things we might do to protect Martin's wife and to retrieve Tawni and his son Ben. As we planned, Jothan drove and was trying to get used to his new Arm and mechanical fingers. The contraption was kind of weird in that his left and right fingers were controlled by his "good" arm, so he could use the hand, but it would grab when the good hand grabbed. Jothan seemed to be getting used to it very well as we neared the city of Cogan where Martin lived up until a few hours ago.

The Palai City of Cogan

Unfortunately, there were very few light skinned people living in the city of Cogan, so it was decided Conrad and Martin would go while the others secured the vehicle and kept it hidden. I could easily transfer from one to the other as needed, provided Conrad was touching Martin, and as was the custom with the people of Palai, Martin walked ahead of his servant.

Escape

It would be a long walk from our vehicle, but we could not risk our vehicle being seen. We did not reach Martin's home for almost 3 hours of walking. If I had actually been there I would have been tired. Finally, we reached his home just before sunrise. Our hope was that if there were guards, they would be asleep.

To view us must have been crazy as Martin took off his clothes while Conrad held his feet and I entered him while he became invisible and stuck his head through the various walls of his house. Let me tell you being inside a person is weird but being inside a person that isn't there is really weird. While I could see, somehow, it was not perfect and it was dark to make it worse, but we found where his wife was and he was right they had a guard in the kitchen waiting for him to return and his wife was in the living room in full view of the Mystifier Guard. Her son was in a different room, upstairs, with a different guard so we had a serious problem. The guard and Ben were both asleep and we found an open window on the second floor. Things were about to get weirder.

We moved to a location where the chain with Conrad, me, and Martin could enter a closet a good distance from the kitchen, where the guard had been. Once he was safely through the wall, I returned to Conrad and together we levitated to the second story window, using information provided by Jack, the demon. There, Conrad entered without incident. As we headed for the room holding his son, Martin had found clothes in the closet, peered out behind the guard who had a plan of his own.

Martin's wife was not from Palai, she was from Hanar and the meeting of Martin and Tawni, is another story sort of like a "Romeo and Juliet" or "Hatfield's and McCoy's", but they loved each other. This guard thought little of the Hanar wife and had decided to have his way with her while he waited. He had already removed his clothes and was almost upon a tied up Tawni. She would not yell so that her son would not be more afraid, but Martin's anger had made its own plan.

Martin quickly came up behind the guard and became invisible. Then he thrust his hand into his head. Momentarily became visible and then becoming invisible again, he quickly removed the damaged appendage. It was a risky move and not without consequence. He became visible again just before leaving the guards lifeless head and the tips of 2 of his fingers became part of the dead man. Blood spewed out of the 2 fingertips and he quickly wrapped them tightly as he untied his wife. He signaled for her to leave and hid outside the back door. She knew enough about her husband to know he knew what he was doing so she got clothes together and was about to go out back, but she stayed by the door just in case.

Making the most of his time, he grabbed the guard's weapon and ran up the stairs.

In the vehicle on the way over, I had been practicing the Mystifier trick and I began vibrating in opposition to Conrad. I'm not sure exactly what I was doing, but it worked while we were in preparation. The idea was for me to be the eyes again, but this time Conrad would walk through a wall. The plan succeeded, but the guard was alerted somehow and went towards Martin's son while drawing his weapon and pointing at us.

Martin had made it up the stairs and threw open the door just as the guard grabbed Ben. The guard fired as Conrad and I quickly ran to Ben and Martin fired to kill the guard, but Martin had been shot, badly.

We made it downstairs with the wounded Martin and Tawni and Conrad, wrapped up his wound and applied substantial pressure. The wound was still bleeding and Tawni was crying and Martin was trying to comfort her. We were about to leave when Martin told us to wait and get a large wooden crate in the garage. Ben was a strapping young man and he and Tawni carried the box and a bag of clothes while Conrad carried Martin to the Guard's vehicle in the front of the yard. Within a matter of minutes, we had made it back near the hiding place of our comrades, ditched the vehicle, and got back to relative safety. After quickly getting inside, Jothan, drove away quietly.

Will There Be Death?

Inside the vehicle was a madhouse as Martin was bleeding, from his fingers and belly, his wife was hysterical and his son was crying, *"Don't leave me Dad!"*

Maria grabbed Ben and told him that she would do whatever she could for him and Jamma quickly removed the trackers from Ben and Tawni. Jamma was a great at doctoring, but this was really bad. It was time for me to try more of the extended reality stuff and help somehow. Conrad was holding Martin so I entered Martin and felt his pain. The bullet was lodged in his liver. While I am no doctor, I was pretty sure a bullet should not be there so I guided Conrad's fingers holding a small loop of wire to the location of the projectile so that Conrad could remove it with the least amount of extra damage. Once it was removed, a hot iron was inserted and used to cauterize the bleeding organ. Let me tell you something about possessing a man's body when he has pain everywhere. It is PAINFUL. I inspected the wound and had him burn another area. I almost thought I would pass out, but Martin was still holding his wife's hand.

Just what I needed, not only was I feeling Conrad's emotions, but also Martins and his wife's. Once the iron was removed, Jamma cauterized the fingertips and inserted a large amount of an antibiotic substance she used in her clinic for treating animals for similar wounds. I stayed "inside" Martin for 2 hours as Conrad and his wife Tawni held onto him. My soul linked with his soul and I gave him assurances and hope. Sometimes hope is the best cure for anything. Tawni cried and cried and I reached into her soul to comfort as best I could. She had been certain the war would kill her husband, but now he could be dying in the relative safety of their invaded home.

It would be most of the following day that the three of us comforted, communicated, wept over, and stayed with Martin. He became fevered after about an hour so we had to cool him down some until he got shivers and Tawni hugged him tightly. We must have done something right because, in the morning, Martin opened his eyes and put his good hand on Tawni's hand. His soul was becoming invigorated and ready to stay with his broken body. I removed myself and went back into Conrad.

We were all exhausted and Maria had guided Jothan to the place near the flying Arc, where we disembarked, covered our vehicle, and took the short trip to our guarded camp. Conrad and Maria had made something to carrying Martin in and we soon reunited with the others. We were all fugitives. OK, I was just a visitor, but these people now felt like my family. Ben had not let go of the weapon Martin had taken since we left the city; the group saw one of the people guarding the location and waved. As we came near the escape craft, I could see a group of people. There were four men and five women. While I would have liked to stay; I had to leave to see if I had made the worst choice of my life.

Back to the Demon

When I got back to my own time, it felt weird because Jack was in my body. He made it known that he was thankful for me letting him stay even for a short time and that he would leave me alone. Initially, I was very relieved. I don't know what I thought I was coming home to, but I was really scared.

"Wait a second", I said, *"You can stay with me a little, provided you do it on my terms."* ----What in the world was I doing?

Jack said, *"Anything you want I will do."*

"I need information and training!" I said, *"I need to know how to keep myself safe when I leave my body and I need to understand how this controlling matter is done; ----and I need to know what you liked to watch on TV."*

Jack agreed and said, *"I can keep your body safe!"* What if you are not around or a more powerful demon or multiple demons try to take control?" I blurted out.

Jack seemed to be saddened when he told me that he had been what was called a *"Principality Demon"* in the Bible. His power was and is substantial and he had commanded many lesser demons and hurt many people long ago, but he, "visited" an old drunk whose name was Max. Little did he know that the man was a true believer and follower of the incarnated Creator, Jesus. *"I tried to turn him"*, Jack said, *"but the more I tried, the more I burned inside. Max could have proclaimed the name of Jesus at any time and have forced me out, but instead, he simply read more and more and prayed more and more and soon, I was wanting him to read and pray and I was turned; not just to keep me from burning during the end of days, but also because I found love in Jesus name.--- Somehow, I was drawn to you as if*

I was supposed to connect with you.-- No other demon would try to come near when I am here."

What if you are not around? I said. He simply said, *"Where would I go?"*

I told him, *"You can't just stay inside me!"*

Jack said, *"I understand, but I meant I will always be near and will leave you alone when you need privacy, like being with a female and whatever."*

I began asking questions and learning all I could in a short period of time.

"Are there other spirits like angels?" --- Jack came back and said, *"Angels were provided carnal bodies when they "Visit", and demons stay away from them. I talked to one a long time ago and the angel told me God loved me, then he disappeared. I don't know if I imagined it or the angel really said that to me, but that simple sentence gave me hope that I might be able to be saved during the last days and even see Jesus."*

"How can I get an unwanted demon to leave?" --- Jack came back and said, *"Trust in God and simply say, in the name of Jesus leave. No demon can stay no matter how powerful, if you truly believe God will remove him or her."*

All this sounded like it was coming from a Church sermon but it was coming from something or someone I had always feared--- a demon---- He almost seemed like a friend.

He could feel my friendship and I could feel his as we watched an old western on the Television. I told my doctor friend, *"Demons really like movies with monsters and anything that brings out excitement."*

After the show I felt hungry and asked Jack what food he liked. He told me, anything spicy. Just as he said that, I got an upset stomach and realized, I should never have left my body without instructions about my sensitive stomach. —We settled on chips and salsa as having a little kick without destroying my guts.

After eating, I took out my Bible to read about the Pleistocene and my computer that had the entire volumes of the Jewish Essene Texts and the Nag Hammadi Jewish Texts. I wanted to know what to expect in the coming catastrophe. Jack commented, how he loved it when people read from the Genesis story during the time when he was alive. I asked him, *"When did you die, exactly?"*

I died during the reign of King Kullassina-bel of Sumeria. He was my brother. This was about 8 thousand years ago. My name was Jacassina-bel, but I shortened it. I think my brother was a good king and we traded with the Shemites to the west. There was a battle for power when my brother died. I was next in line but I was killed by my uncle Nangishlishma and I have been in sort of a limbo ever since.

I found a chart showing how the "Giants of old" had become "angels"; how many were turned back into humans called Anak. I also found many details about how they became demons.

I showed my Doctor, a chart I made, showing how the demons came into being and how they came from the humans known as Anak along with a second one of the Sumerian and Assyrian king timelines showing when Jack's brother ruled 8 thousand years ago. Since Cindy saw them, I thought they would be useful to you.

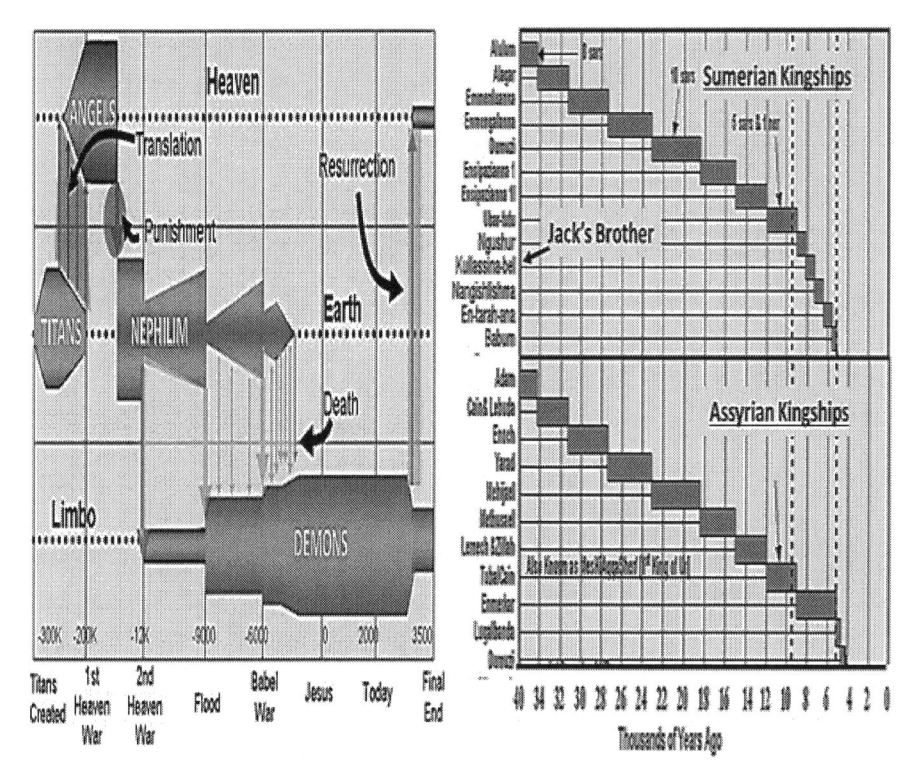

Jack suddenly became sad and said, *"Do you think I will be able to get to Heaven if I trust in God."* I told him, *"Let's see what the ancient texts say."* I pulled up some of the texts on demons and showed him some positive remarks including one made by a great Anak ruler named Thoth.

Enoch 15:8-12- *And now, the giants, who are produced from the spirits* [Angels that became Anak] *and flesh, they shall become evil spirits [demons] upon the earth, and on the earth shall be their dwelling until the great resurrection time. Evil spirits have proceeded from their bodies;*

Matthew 24- *But, anyone who stands firm to the end of the Tribulation wars will be saved.*

Daniel 12:10-Many shall purify themselves, *and make themselves white, and be refined and be saved;*

Our Great Power:23 *And <u>I [God] shall withdraw with everyone who will know me and not cause condemnation.</u>*

Emerald Tablet [Thoth]- *There are two regions between this life and God, traveled by the Souls who depart from this Earth; the first is the home of illusion [limbo]. The second one Heaven. Three guard the way; they turn back the souls of unworthy men. Beyond them lies Heaven and God. There, when my work among men has been finished, will <u>I, Thoth, join those in heaven.</u>*

I told Jack, *"This is saying Thoth, who was an Anak, was able to go to heaven after death."*

Jack said, *"You know, I knew Thothinica-tim, who went by Thoth, when he ruled the Land of Egypt. He was a great man and one who stayed true to God even when he ruled. I was not so good. My brother and I both worshipped the great Beelzebub who had died before my time and controlled many demons. At least, I thought he was great at the time. He is the one you call Satan. After I died, I was really mad that men from the lineage of Adam did not have to become demons. I did so much harm. I caused the painful death of many men who tried to worship the Creator and those who worshipped Beelzebub. I really had no preference. I only wanted to experience life at its fullest and never have to go back into "limbo." After a minute, Jack blurted out, "Now I'm trying to make amends, but I don't think I can ever make up for my evilness."*

Soon Jack was making me cry, so I tried to comfort him. I said, "None of us are good in the eyes of God, but we don't have to be. God Incarnate, came to become man, to die for your sins and my sins and then return to heaven to help guide us to be the best we can by trying to do the will of God."

Jack said to my mind, *"I'm trying my best, but it is really hard. I know there will be some type of horrible punishment by Beelzebub for my actions at some time, but I just don't care. His evil and desire to destroy as many people as possible is just wrong."*

I said, *"I am certain that if he does confront you simply call on the name of Incarnate God just like you told me to do. That's essentially what King Thoth was saying and he probably meant the words for you."*

Cindy was crying again. What kind of psychologist starts crying during a session? She said, *"I never thought about how a demon might feel---was he tricking you?"*

I said, *"No he really felt that way. I can get him so you can ask him yourself if you like."*

"Never mind, just be careful," she reminded me again.

After the mothering, I went back to my story.

"For 2 days, Jack helped me understand the ways of demons, soul transfer, ways to keep from having unwanted visitors, and ways to use and expand the capabilities of my host. I could wait no longer and I grabbed the stupid stone purse to return."

Collection

When I got back, it had been another year. For a full year the "fugitives" had not only survived, but they had filled the craft with all types of things they would need to not only survive the Extinction Period, but also to rebuild life.

The adventurers included Conrad (Biologic Designer) and his wives, Maria (the horticulturalist who was now the mother of a three year old girl) and Lily; Jothan (Botanist) and his wives, Jamma (a skilled veterinarian who would become their doctor) and Susan (a genuinely great musician, who was now pregnant); the Magnetic Engineer, Reese, and one of his wives, Bonnie, (who now had a three year old boy); and Bartlet, who, among other things, was a great pilot. He was still holding out for his wife and son to go with them. Bartlet would leave every 2 days to a known place away from the hidden ship and wait to see if they would join the group.

Martin the Mystifier, his wife, Tawni, and their son Ben had joined the group, but these outsiders still were cause for some concern. These 14 would soon be 15 whenever Susan had her baby.

I had been talking and talking and I realized Dr. Cindy was drooping. I paid for the massive amounts of coffee and we both left. As we were leaving, I accidentally kissed her on the cheek. She could not hide she was getting emotional feelings for me and I had violated her trust. I also saw a deep secret.

She seemed to ignore my mistake and indicated we should continue tomorrow. She turned around to leave and told me to stay away from demons. Then she stopped, turned around and kissed me, with purpose.

I didn't know what to do, I certainly didn't want to ruin her life and my life, certainly, was messed up. In my mixed-up set of motions, I told her, *"Thank you,"* then I said, *"Tomorrow it is!"*. I turned around to go to my car, stopped, turned back around, kissed her again, and then quickly apologized.

"What an idiot!", I thought—Jack agreed.

"What are you doing here?", I said in my head. Jack apologized and said, *"I just had to make a comment---I'm gone."*

Cindy had no knowledge of what was going on in my head as she made the next session place her home.

We both left.

Soon my phone rang and Cindy was on the line and she apologized for her unprofessional action and I told her it was my fault and apologized again. *"Tomorrow will be a new day",* she said and that was followed by *"Goodnight J-man"*.

From nowhere, I heard, *"Sorry"*. OK! Jack, I said, come on out and let's get some food. *"What would you like?"*

He came back with *"Hot wings."* I punished him with unsalted chicken pot pie. *"What are we watching?"*, he said as I finished my last bite. I started to say "Mr. Rogers", but my hand was guided to one of the Star Wars tapes. Sometimes it can be challenging to have a demon in your head. Lucky for him, that's what I really wanted to see so we blasted off into space—on the TV.

Sunday came soon and Jack was gone so I called and headed out to my next session. The sky was dreary, but I was excited to see my doctor and to continue my story as I left off in a bad place.

I got to her home, knock on the door, and she greeted me with such a smile that the day brightened. She had made brunch and it was good too!

After eating, I helped with the dishes and we took coffee into the living room. She took out her computer this time as she was simply making too many notes for a writing pad and the audio recordings just seemed too clinical. After she was set up, she said, *"Do you remember where you were?"* I told her *"Yes"*, and I started from our last discussion.

Bartlet's Son

Conrad told the group I was back again and Conrad introduced me to everyone, including Bartlet. He was extremely troubled and said, *"I don't know if I can make the trip if I have to leave my wife, Anne. I haven't even seen her in over a year."*

Conrad, on his own, said, *"Let's go find her."*

He knew that Bartlet would never forgive himself if he left and there was any chance he could take his family. We tried to make the trip back to the city with as few people as we could, but Bartlet had to go, Jothan came along as driver, in case there was trouble and Lily came along. Her other husband had been a supervising agent for war supplies just like Bartlet's son, and we did not know if that would be helpful or not. When we got to the city, Bartlet showed Jothan where to park the vehicle and we were on foot. Jothan stayed with the vehicle while Conrad, Bartlet, and Lily [and me] went to his home.

 I was not going to be an easy "hi/bye" sort of thing.

Retrieval

Peering through several windows, we were pretty sure the home was empty and we entered. Once inside, Bartlet called his wife's number and she answered. She was with her other husband, Duke who was a contractor. Ever since Bartlet, sort of vanished, and the massive flood, Venus destruction, and a famine that was now starting to hit the supermarket, Duke had asked her to stay close to "home". Bartlet asked if there was any way for her to meet him, she said yes and he told her he was at their home about 2 blocks away.

It wasn't long before the front doorknob was moving and in came Anne along with her other husband, Duke. While Duke was a good "friend" of Bartlet, there was panic around the room. Immediately after they entered, Conrad grabbed Duke by the arm and I "enter him" for a check. It was hard to tell his thoughts as he was filled with confusion, anger, concern and, deep love for his wife all at the same time. Soon, he began to settle down and he hugged Bartlet as soon as he could get close enough and his wife quit kissing. Lily jumped in and began kissing Duke, and all his anger and confusion had turned to the familiar affection I was used to sensing.

I began investigating Duke's intension and found that he had become a believer after all of the catastrophes and they had even visited Noah. The problem was their son or Bartlet's son---I don't know which one. Anyway, Shepard, had been sent into the war to support fighting down south. As far as I could tell, we were near Iran so they were possibly talking about India. Both of

Shephard's parents—now all three were worried sick and had been trying to figure out how to get to him during most of the past 6 months. Bartlet, almost crying, said to Anne, *"Do you think you can go with us?"* Duke jumped in and said, *"We both want to come with you if you will take me also. —but we need to find out about Shepard. If he wants to come or if he thinks he must stay."*

His last letter had talked about God and conversion and things that gave them hope, but they knew the Military did those sorts of things to find rebels and eliminate them. After reading Shephard's letter, each of the new team decided we were off to India (or wherever he was fighting). While we had enough room for the 6 of us, as I took no room at all, we decided we would take 2 vehicles. Our flying vehicle would be augmented with a truck that would be driven by Duke.

At first, I didn't even think about Pleistocene people using massive land vehicles for travel, but then I remembered in Central Turkey and on the Islands of Malta, now separated from the European coastline. Both had identical indications of extremely heavy 10-inch-wide tired trucks of some kind all over the place.

Cindy stopped me and asked, *"What are you talking about? The only thing I remember about the Pleistocene in school was the Flintstone cars."* I decided the best way to explain was with actual Archeological finds. Vehicle impressions showed vehicles about the same size as modern ones with 10-inch-wide tires that wore ruts into the roads because of extremely heavy loads. Some tracks showed an external gear-drive to assist moving heavy loads. As always what I showed Cindy I am showing here. The first row was a sampling of the Turkish tire tracks turned into solid rock over thousands of years, depicting 6 to 10 foot wide super heavy vehicles.

The second set was of massive tire tracks encased in stone and found on the Island of Malta, near Italy, from when they had been part of the mainland during the Pleistocene.

Besides the petrified tire tracks, I showed her some type of regularly spaced "cog imprints" between the tires, showing the loads were so heavy, secondary "climbing" devices on the trucks were sometimes used in the Pleistocene.

Duke would have to be our GPS as the satellites would not be up for another 10-thousand years. He knew where we were going and was not wanted by authorities. He and Anne took the land route and we flew overhead through the night and tried to stay hidden.

Before we left, Anne told us that when they saw Noah, he claimed the destruction could happen at any time, so we had better hurry and he told us something strange about Conrad. Anne followed up with, *"Is he possessed?"*

Conrad said, *"It's nothing like that! James came back from the future and is using my body to share my experience."* I was introduced and got more of the same- *"What is the future like?"* questions and then we were off.

By morning we had crossed the desert and we were in India, but Duke continued. Within a couple of hours, he slowed and parked his truck near a small stream deep in the central portion of India. We all got out and he said from here on, it can only be me and Shepard's mom. Conrad explained why he and I needed to go with them so the 4 of us or three and a half set off to the checkpoint with Conrad stuffed in the back. Without incident we were on base and parked. Conrad got out and we went to the dorm where her son was staying. He was called and within a very short time, Shepard appeared in the front "lobby".

The checking Sargent was near Conrad so he grabbed his arm, and I made a suggestion that he really needed to go to the bathroom and get a cigarette. He told Shepard's parents that he would give them some 'alone time'. While Conrad had his arm, I found out they had been there for about a week and would be leaving tomorrow morning to fight the leader of rebels who had claimed the southern portion of India. The Sargent told us not to stay long and made his apologies as Shepard was hugging his mom, his dad, and his great uncle Conrad almost at the same time. I had entered Shepard and found he was full of fear, but more importantly, he wanted to leave this misery and find life anywhere else.

Now all we had to do is leave, get by the check gate, travel hundreds of miles without anyone knowing, and get back to safety--- and one more thing. The Sargent was returning. I had Shepard appear to be getting horribly sick. He was a great actor. He was about to call for assistance, but I fed him a thought that his family could take him to the makeshift hospital. We left quickly and the Sargent thanked us for helping him out.

Somehow, Conrad had been recognized and a group of soldiers were on their way to take control of him. We were almost at our getaway vehicle when the alarm rang out. I told him to find one of the soldiers that was alone and capture him. Conrad told everyone to stay hidden and we soon came upon what appeared to be a high-ranking soldier.

Unfortunately for him, he was alone and was grabbed. Conrad had super strength, due to my demon training and he/we subdued the Officer without incident. Soon he was tied, gagged, and hidden. Oh yes! He did not have his clothes. Conrad had now become the captive which required one more specialty. As I prepared Conrad for what was about to happen, he began to scream and I made his vocal cords too tight for sound. The discomfort was quickly over, but Conrad felt strange. I told him we needed to find the others. We began to make our way back but tried to not draw attention. Two soldiers came nearby and both stopped and saluted. Conrad saluted back and they departed.

He had the face of the captured man. It wasn't perfect, but no one looks directly at a general. We quickly found the hidden group and Shepard went white trying to explain some ridiculous thing about going to the hospital when Conrad stopped him and told him he was his uncle. Shepard, Anne, and Duke all fell on the ground and then they began giggling almost out of control for a couple of seconds until Conrad snapped them out of it. I was pretty busy right now, so they had to make it back through the gate without my assistance, but when the guards saw the new Conrad, they allowed our group to leave without incidence.

Back to the vehicle and then back to the other vehicle and then the long trip back to our rescue ship involved many explanations and quite a bit of laughter. Lily cut out Shepard's tracker and we threw it down into a raging river.

Large Group

Now the group had grown to 17 not including me and Lily took me aside and told Conrad, that he promised she would be able to have sex whenever I came back. While this sounds awkward, the sexual habits of this group were what you would have to call "sharing" as Bartlet's wife and Bartlet also joined in.

Did I tell you that when there are deep sensations, they a doubled for me and the host and those that are touched have more reserve energy than they would have normally? It would take 2 hours before the "session" to be officially ended and we all came out to the living area to claps and hugs.

Conrad had some explaining to do. How was he someone else? How did he overtake the commander of the Army unit so easily and how did he convince the Sargent to leave? Lily giggled but good old Martin came close and told him he knew the answers and he might be the best to tell as Conrad's alter-ego had been the reason he, his wife, and boy were all with the group. He said, *"I owe my life to the man inside Conrad whose name is James."* -----

Soon everyone was hugging and asking me specific questions about my future home. As an afterthought, Maria looked outside and it was raining.

It looked like final preparations were about to begin. I know I should have left as it had now been almost three full days, but I had to make sure these people would be safe as the first part of this extinction was going to be horrible.

The Flood

I stopped for a short rest and I could see the confusion in Cindy. I'm sure all this seemed scary to her, but now, more than ever, I wanted her to know me; not only to help me battle my demons;---OK! wrong choice of words; but also I really wanted her to help me be nicer and; I think, I was having feelings for her.

Cindy just said, *"So, did you have fun with those two women?"*

I explained that Lily was trying to get pregnant and I believe that was a major motive for Anne as well. I may be the main reason I was sent to them so life could be renewed in the Holocene Age.

Cindy shrugged, and said, *"Do you want a cookie?"*

I, initially, ignored her request about one of the great cookies, and told her the flood was nothing like many of the religions describe as they never read the companion texts. The entire earth was about to shift about 30 degrees according to what the 'Hawaiian-Island-hotspot-track' did, 10 thousand years ago. The Magnetic signature provided by the continuous eruptions in the center of the Atlantic Ocean showed a massive magnetic field change as well as did many, many texts. This shift would cause massive and abrupt changes in weather, and all the water at the poles would melt and begin to refreeze at a new location. Over a million Mammoths were eating in a flower filled field when the earth shift made Siberia in the Arctic Circle which froze them solid with flowers still in their mouths. The Rain, Flood, and unbelievable shock of the earth shift wasn't all, as tidal waves over a mile high would cover mountains and kill everyone. I showed here the hotspot track of Hawaii as it traveled all over the Pacific and made a 40 degree shift 10 thousand years ago. Here is the track for you as well.

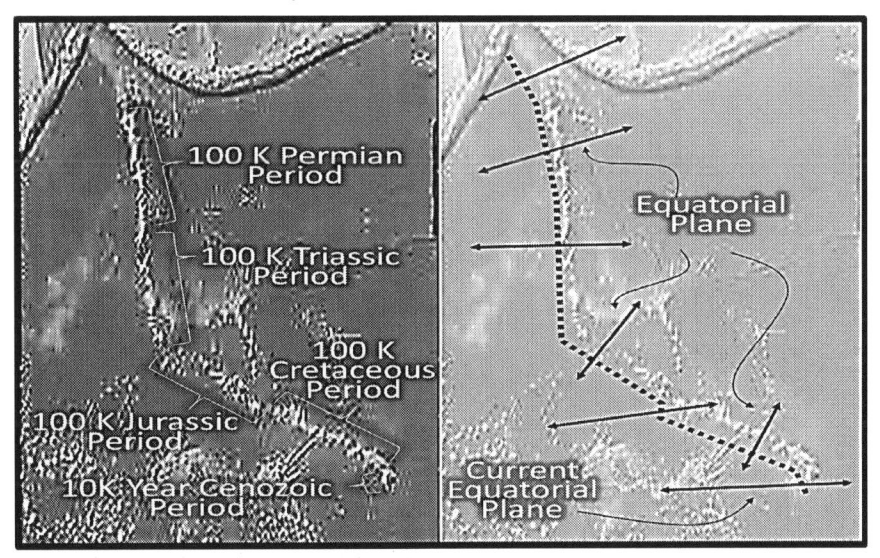

She simply said, *"If that was true, why are we not told about it?"* By now I was sure she already knew, but I told her religious dogma and consensus science had hidden the truth for thousands of years. I could not tell if she was just taunting me or was mad at me, but I took one of the cookies.

After taking a sip of coffee and scarfing down a peanut butter and coconut cookie made by a psychologist, friend, woman, great cook, person; I continued and she continued writing on her computer that seemed like it was about to catch fire. I think I saw her smile a little, but she might have been mad and I hoped for her understanding.

"Outside, the rain was getting harder. Hail hit hard against the hull and lightning sounded like a war zone. The flying roadster was securely attached to the bottom of the Escape Arc; the engines were turned on and tested; the people quickly took seats and strapped in for a rough take off; a group prayer began as the rain got harder and harder. One of the small portal windows was smashed in by ice and the rain came in sideways from the opening. Quite a few tears filled the eyes of the adventurers knowing they could not take many of their friends who would perish. Fear about what came next added to the deep sorrow, but Conrad stayed focused as he believed he had to.

We waited for the water to cover the base of the ship to make take-off easier and the ship rose into the sky. Just as the ship left the surface, massive earthquakes could be heard above the storming rain. Then we all heard the external aircraft mounting give way and the vehicle was dangling as all hell had broken free below. The ship was slammed back and forth by the unbelievable winds but Conrad knew they needed the vehicle for when the land was again solid. He jumped up quickly and I decided to go with him. OK! I had to, but I needed to ensure he was safe.

Four of the clamps were still secure but two had broken away and the broken clamp was dangling in the air. Bartlet was a great pilot and tried to hold the ship as still as possible, but there was no reference below.

There was some heavy strapping material secured to the wall but the vehicle was just out of reach. As Conrad stretched, I stretched him some more so that he could grab the precious cargo and his additional strength allowed him to secure one side very quickly. The other side was simply too hard to attach so I tried the last thing my demon friend had taught me. Conrad noticed that the motions were getting slower. What was actually happening was Conrad's mind was temporarily going faster. It probably was fun to watch him move like this, but I was way too busy concentrating on the actions I needed to do to keep him focused, keep him strong, and keep him working fast enough.

With all that on my mind, I am not sure what he did, but the vehicle was again attached securely.

For safety, Conrad placed another strap to secure the tail section and we returned to the other passengers. The ship did not sound like it would survive the onslaught of the wind, lightning, hail and torrential rain and it was creaking and moaning like a sick animal. Many were crying, and sobbing, but Maria was simply praying out loud. Soon, there was a calm from somewhere. I'm pretty sure it came from God, but it was amazing. As the ship was still tossed almost to the breaking point, I remembered what the books of Jasher and Enoch indicated Noah went through and what the Sumerian texts indicated the Anak went through. Here are their words.

Jasher -6:11-32 *the Lord caused the whole Earth to shake, and the sun darkened, and the <u>foundations of the world raged, and the whole Earth was moved violently, and the lightning flashed, and the thunder roared, and all the fountains in the Earth were broken up,</u> all the living creatures within the Ark <u>were turned about like pottage in a cauldron</u>.*

Enoch 64, 67, 80- *Noah saw that the Earth <u>became inclined</u> and that destruction approached. -The Earth labors and is <u>violently shaken</u>. Surely, I shall perish with it. -<u>There was a great perturbation on the earth</u>. [Earth Shift] --this <u>water shall change and become cold</u>. [Earth shift] And all things on the Earth shall alter, and <u>shall not appear in their time: fruits of the Earth shall be backward, and shall not grow in their time, And the moon shall not appear at her time</u>. [Earth Shift]*

Sumerian Flood-*The Anak [called Annunaki by the Sumerians] controlled the world before the flood. An ark was built and the <u>seed of every animal</u> was transported. <u>Above the Earth, the Anak cried out in fear</u>.*

Soon we were exceedingly high and still the escape craft tossed us about. We knew death was below for almost everyone and everything. We were witnessing the Pleistocene Extinction. Millions and millions of people and animals were all being crushed, or drowned, or frozen. Pile of animals became twisted together and are still found today that way

As soon as I thought the ship was out of harm's way, massive--- no------ much more than massive tidal waves could be seen far below, crushing everything in front of it. It was hard to believe Noah would survive. I could imagine his Ark flipping and righting itself as wave after wave of tidal action and torrential rain filled the entire world. The very atmosphere was like a cyclone spinning us like a top. I was so very glad Bartlet and his piloting skills were on this trip. But I had to leave as something didn't feel right.

Demonic Cooking

I told Conrad to tell them I will see them again and I was back home. Smoke was everywhere and I was outside talking to a fireman. The Kitchen had a fire and I, or Jack, had been explaining that he overloaded the electric circuit and a greasy frying pan left on the stovetop had caught fire. The grease spilled on to the floor, causing more and more flames and massive amounts of smoke.

Never leave a demon in your body too long!!!!

Cindy broke in and said, *"I knew that demon would be trouble. That's why they are called demons."* Then she said,*" So, what happened? Did you lose your home?"*

Jack's Fire

I continued. "It didn't take the firemen too long to put out the fire, but if Jack had kept the place cleaner, none of this would have happened. A fireman told me I would have to find a place to stay for a few weeks for the damage to get repaired. He handed me a card of someone that could help repair the damage kitchen. It was him and his brother. Just imagine a fireman repairing a fire damaged home---- It seemed odd to me, but I told him to give me an estimate and we would talk in the morning. I got some clothes and headed for a motel.

Once I got to my room, I called out for Jack, who, not surprisingly, was quiet. When he finally did speak, it was in massive phrases of apology, I told him he promised to keep my body safe and look what happened. I must say after seeing the world get destroyed, this little kitchen fire was not nearly as earth shattering as it would have been." I almost chuckled as I thought how petty I was thinking some smoke in my kitchen was anything worth worrying about while most of the planet was being destroyed just hours before--- in my reality.

"Please don't send me away", Jack cried. I just told him you can stay if you tell me about how his ancestors were saved through the worldwide flood.

Cindy said, *"I think you are getting to chummy with this demon. Please be careful. I can't help you if you bring on the whole demonic group; and I am going to help you—I swear."*

New Revelation

I shrugged off Dr. Cindy's concerns politely and continued. As this next part of my story was very important.

"Jack was more than happy to tell about his early years when he was alive. They were the memories that kept him from going completely crazy like many of the demons who had become vengeful, and ugly souls filled with hate and loathing." These were Jacks words not mind---directly.

My first question in this new pursuit was, *"Just how many Anak people lived during the Pleistocene?"*

"While I thought he would simply say a bunch, his answer was surprising. He said, *"While you would not think I would know that answer, as a small child, I was told the Anak had a census taken just before the Pleistocene Extinction. It was an attempt to divide lands in some way to halt the killing and proclaim lands, but notice was sent out and it was determined that around the world, according to what I remember, was a total of 2 million, 198 thousand, and 4. I suppose I remembered the number for thousands of years because of the tiny 4 at the end."* My father told me quite a few had died before the census, especially those stationed or living on Venus had all passed away when it just blew up one day.

How Many Demons

If you are really asking how many demons there are, I would have to guess almost double that number. While we can contact each other it's not like having a person or an animal nearby, we are all just tormented souls. Communication is by might, not words. As there is nothing to sense in limbo, we rely on most communication after possessing another "live" human.

Living in a Pig

One time something like a hundred other demons and I had entered a man and made him do all types of things. Even with the cramped level of confinement in his body, it was much better than being "NOWHERE". The Incarnated Creator came along and commanded us to all leave. It was like knife blades slashing us free from the poor man. As we ran away, we saw a herd of pigs and entered them briefly, but they ran into a lake and died, so we, very quickly were back in the horrors of nothingness.

I stopped Jack and asked excitedly, *"You met Jesus?"*

Jack almost trembled when he answered. *"There is no doubt about the Creator yanking me and those with me out of that man as we were desperately trying to experience some semblance of life again. For some time, I was really mad at God all over. For hundreds of years, I made life miserable for many people. It would be centuries before I understood, my problems were made by me not God and certainly not because of those who were so very fortunate that their souls would sleep after death. The Anak Army was cursed by God because of the War in Heaven as our General whose name was Gadrael, or Satan, pushed the Anak to take control of Heaven and allow carnal things like sex, getting power over others, fighting, and getting even."* My great grandfather had been in that war so he was a demon well before the time I died. For about a year, my great-granddad possessed me and convinced me that the creator God was horrible and his punishment was not bearable.

Description of Heaven by an Anak

My great-granddad told me that the place God made for the ancients when they became released spirits, or angels, was a beautiful place, but God would not allow angels to obtain power of any reasonable level as he wanted to control everything. He also would not allow the basic needs of humans like hatred, greed, and sex. In fact, he didn't even give angels parts needed for such encounters. He also complained about how it was always daytime and how God was everywhere. While he complained I could tell it must have been a beautiful place, but his bitterness was pushed into me during his possession. When he finally released me and found a new mark, I was a horrible mess.

My mom was an Adamic hybrid from a northern clan. She told me she was drawn to the grandeur of the city loved my dad and had my brother and me. I was just as cursed as my great-grandfather, grandfather, and my dad, and I have no idea what happened to my mom.

"Wait a minute. What was Jesus like?" I yelled.

Jesus Described by a Demon

Jack could somehow tell, my mind was more centered on God incarnate, than his family, so Jack began describing what he remembered of God incarnate, 2 thousand years ago. *"He was like a massive shining light, filled with warmth and beauty and I was not able to get near him. At first, I wanted to get near him, as he emanated love somehow. But the others wanted to stand against him and we all ended up in pigs. As he spoke, all of us were frozen and each time he talked it burned. We had no choice but to comply with whatever Jesus said.* Jack also said, *"I know one thing about Jesus; you guys don't have him pictured right. Moses wrote down strict rules about how all Jews were to wear their hair.*

***Leviticus 21 and 27**- You shall not shave the top of your head, nor shave the sides of your beard. You shall not cut the hair on the sides of your head or trim your beard.*

All of the religious Jews had scraggly beards as required to show they were Jewish. The scragglier the better. Jesus looked like most of the others. He had a bushy head of hair and a wild curly beard. Except for this power that emanated from him, he looked like a fisherman.

The Demoness, Lilith

My second question was about "Lilith". According to many ancient Jewish texts, she was not only Adam's first wife but also, she became a nasty and powerful demoness after death. Moses tried to eliminate the worship of Lilith as a "goddess" by limiting what he wrote about her, but Moses did mention that sometime after Adam was made, Adam got lonely because his "helpmeet" Lilith, had gone and he went around looking at various animals for companionship before God cloned another woman to be his new helpmeet/wife. Without the other Jewish texts, it appeared that God had forgotten to make a woman, but the weirdest thought is that God thought that Adam could find a meaningful relationship with a cow. Anyway, I asked Jack if Lilith was a real Anak human.

Adam's First Wife

Jack became serious and said, *"Don't mess around with that demoness. She is just as powerful as me, but she truly hates all the "lesser humans" as she says. The stories in the Jewish texts are true for the most part except for the taking of children. No demon can take a child. There is some type of protection from God. As far as Lilith being mated with Cain, I was told that did happen and that allowed the Anak people to have children by partial-Cro-Magnon hybrids like my mother, so I guess you could say I have a bit of "lesser human" in me."*

Genesis 2:18-20- *[After Lilith left] God said, "It is not good for the man to be alone. I will make [another] help-meet suitable for him." He brought the animals to Adam but for Adam no suitable help-meet was found.*

For you readers; this did not mean God thought Adam should marry a skunk. Because Eve had a hybrid child, Lilith was the first Anak, able to have children by Cro-Magnon.

Zohar 1:19 *The Serpent had intercourse with Eve and Cain was born. She could not attach herself to him, but later, she approached him and bore [those who would become] demons. She roams the world to afflict men with disease and kills children.*

These things were being confirmed by Jack.

Anak During the Pleistocene

Then I said to Jack, *"Tell me about the days before and during the Pleistocene Extinction."* So, Jack began telling me more of what his great-grandfather and his father told him.

Massive Environmental Destructions- *"Just before the Pleistocene Extinction, our outpost on Venus was destroyed and it seemed to rain pieces of its moon for many days on the Earth"*. Most sane people stayed inside during those days and many lands were set on fire, this also brought on flooding around the world. There was fear that God himself was doing the destruction."

A Rouge Group and Civil War- *"One group of Anak called Nephadim in your books, were different in that they could reproduce with "lesser humans"* (I knew he was talking about the Cro-Magnon here and I felt him smile for his joke). *Their offspring were infertile, but they were huge and mean and they ate people. I'm not sure how all this went down, but during all the calamities, the Nephadimics began a separate civil war and* began killing each other. Within 100 years, or so, of war, all the Nephadim, and all their ravenous children had been killed. I think this was before the Census, and there were about a hundred thousand of these rouges."

Genetics- *"My Granddad ran one of three major genetic investigation companies. I think he had a partner who was one of the Nephadim, but I'm not sure. He had many non-Anak working for him to ensure the Anak people could extend life and could manufacture animals that could be beneficial to us. While he investigated what he believed would help society, the others were modifying humans to make freaks. A number of modified apes were continuously modified to make a new type of humans, but these got more and more bizarre. I don't really remember what they made besides the whale, but they were always getting in trouble with a group called the genetic oversight committee. This just meant they had to pay a fine and say they were sorry or some stupidity like that."*

Anak and the Flood

I wondered if Conrad had worked in Jack's great-grandfather's plant, but I stopped Jack for a minute and said, *"All this is great stuff. Right now, I was trying to find out what happened DURING the Pleistocene Extinction flood."*

Jack apologized for rambling and he said, that was a time his dad said his grandfather wanted to forget. Then he began again. *"My dad told me it was in the spring that the rains began that would spell the end. Many had made preparations, but few, understood the horrors of what was to come. Luckily, my granddad had a friend who was a believer. This guy tried his best to get us to understand, but, it's hard to think of yourself as nothing when you believe you are so powerful. All that was going to change very quickly. The guy---I can't remember his name but I think it started with an "M", --maybe Marduk? Anyway, he told my dad what Noah had been describing and just to be prepared, we had been building an escape ship that could orbit Earth for a time. About 5 Anak families and 5 families of the family of Cain were part of this effort. I suppose the total was about 40 individuals. While others were building bigger and bigger bomb shelters, thinking the war was about to escalate, my granddad and his friends were doing the opposite. Filled with food and supplies, when the rains began, they crowded into the ship. A number of other families came to investigate, but they were sure their shelters would secure them better in case nuclear and magno-blastic bombs were coming. My grandparents and the others closed up the ship as rain was pouring down so hard, you could not see your hand in front of you face. They tried lifting off just as massive earthquakes broke the ground open and tilted the craft. There was no certainty they could build a magnetic bubble to lift us at the extreme angle, but they began the process.*

It was no use, the ship would not rise but the continued the lift process as a massive earthquake almost shook the ship apart, my granddad's arm was cut so badly that blood squirted across the room. Another woman was crushed as straps holding building materials broke free. Then the ground under us opened wider causing a gaseous rupture in the earth and massive clouds of smoke filled the air, but this also righted the ship so the magnetic bubble could allow for the ship to rise. Lightning hit the ship dozens of times and some of the electronics were failing, including all our tracking and mapping systems. Their craft continued to rise.

The plan was to place the craft into an orbit to wait out the storm, but they had no idea what was going to be the extent of it. My dad said they heard a massive moan just before the earth below them sounded like a blast from and thousand cannons. This blast caused the ship to twist and dive as the magnetic field of the entire Earth was disrupted. The pilots tried to convert to airfoil flight, but that didn't work, so they glided downwards the magnetic field shift halted and they were almost out of room when the craft began lifting once again.

For a brief time, they could see below, everything was gone. The oceans had waves as high as mountains and no lights could be seen. The water was as black as soot and their ship was bouncing around like it was sailing in the waters of the storm itself. They rose higher and higher, but their navigation tools were all gone. Higher still and the air became thin so their breathing suits were put on and my granddad's arm was wrapped his new bride who was pregnant with my dad."

Early Flight

I showed Jack some of the space ships etched into walls or carved into effigies from around the ancient world, so I have it next for you as well. I asked what his ship most looked like. He said the image from India and the air-suits were probably similar to second one on the bottom row.

From the Jewish Sacred book "Generations of Adam", I read a short section so Cindy would have a chance at believing how very important flying machines were to the ancient Pleistocene societies. *Timnor [Adam's child] built great engines with which to deface his Mother Earth.* With other machines, his people *flew through the air like birds and explored the depths of the lakes* and rivers. *He also created great instruments of destruction with which his people attacked the people of Cain*, this *led to war and destruction*, Ammah [his wife/sister] *created new forms of beings. [unclean animals]*

160

The Indian representation seemed to be similar to the one that Conrad and his family would escape on.

I put on the "Exorcist" movie and we watched and I felt him giggling from time to time, but other times, he must have remembered something from his past and almost made me cry out. Then we slept.

I had to call the insurance company in the morning I thought. Then I bonked myself in the head and said to Jack, *"Don't burn down my house anymore."* Then I laughed to make sure Jack didn't feel any worse.

Cindy stopped me again and said, *"I'm sorry for my inappropriate worrying, but I think demons are like leprechauns and genies, they get you to hope for things you can't have so they can devastate you."*

I came over and touched her on the arm and I instantly knew she was terrified about the demon and there was something else that haunted her.

"Please believe me when I tell you, Jack is more like a guardian Angel than the descriptions you hear about demons. I truly believe God sent him to me to help me help those that may need my specialty", I said to try to comfort her. *I knew that the Bible indicated that we need to guard against the enemy, meaning demonic enemy, but this guy seems to truly believe in the creator as a savior rather than a warden."*

I tried to explain to her that this whole story happened years ago and since then, Jack has helped me more and more. I did not tell her Jack was with me today and he agreed with all that she was saying knowing how he used to be.

"Do you know how hard it is to carry on a conversation when another conversation is going on in your head????"

Cindy's Demon

I got serious and asked her, *"What else is troubling you so very much?"*

She said, *"The guy with the ears almost haunts me!"*

At first, I thought she still had feelings for the good-looking rock climber with an ear issue, but when I touched her I felt terror.

I asked if it would be alright for me to touch her again and she agreed reluctantly.

Anger, fear, and confusion- I was seeing a woman who was just as messed up as I was. The man's name was Tom and he was a pretty famous rock climber—some type of champion; but he had a mean side. Tom had dated Cindy for almost a year before he brought out his true nature. One evening, she had a bad day and would not see him. She went to bed early and there was a knock on the door.

I know I could have asked her for the details, but my way is so much faster and uninhibited that I thought it would be the easiest for Cindy.

She knew the things I had gotten from her and she began to weep, but I needed to find out the details.

Cindy, at the front door, opened up to her drunken boyfriend. He not only smelled of booze, but also of perfume. He must have been rejected and he came inside forcibly and knocked Cindy to the ground and made her do almost unimaginable things. She scratched at his eyes and he hit her in the stomach almost making her throw up. Finally, the event ended and Tom told her he would see her in the morning.

Cindy called the cops who came over to investigate. After checking on Tom, one returned and told her they saw no evidence of abuse except for the large scar across his face.

Remember, Tom was famous and well liked, and Cindy was a nobody who seemed to be trying to sully the name of an American Icon.

Cindy was in the shower when Tom called and told her she remembered the evening wrong and that he was sorry she took things the wrong way. He then asked if he could see her the following day.

She threw the phone across the room and went to bed. The next morning, her phone rang and Tom was asking about their date. She hung up and for a solid week he attempted to get back with his "mistress". She changed phones, moved into another apartment and finally into another town to forget her shame, hurt, fear, and disbelief in a system that would allow that to happen.

It had been only a matter of seconds and I knew she needed me as much as I needed her right them.

"Tell me what you would like me to do!", I said.

"I just want to forget it!" Cindy said as she was fully in tears by this time.

I said, *"What if I could give him a piece of his own dirty work without hurting him too badly?"*

She came back with indignation and said, *"NO!"*, just as soon as she said it the hurt brought her to her senses. *"What have you got in mind?"* she said.

"What if his fame becomes his downfall? What if things get out about his unusual sexual preferences or methods, or something about how he cheats in competition or something like that? He would have the shame and fear, and loss of respect, but he still would not be harmed."

"How will he know this came from me as retribution?", she blurted out. *"I'm not saying I would go along with such a thing, but when would you do this errand?"*

I told her my students are all in process of doing a finals project and I could take off a day or two. Substitution would be easy, and I know who could take my class. She said, *"I suppose we could call it therapy for me!"* -----I agreed.

Retribution

I made arrangements for a friend to take my class and a showed up on Cindy's front doorsteps Monday around noon. She was ready to go and got in my car. We were off to Philadelphia.

Cindy was holding my hand and she was shaking and said, *"Why are you doing this for me?"*

I told her she was more than a friend to me and I needed to give Jack something to do besides burning down my house.

She hit me on the head and exclaimed, "You *brought that demon!"*

I said, *"You'll see, he can be very helpful and I have gotten pretty good at using his special talents to right some pretty bad wrongs."*

"It still makes me nervous," she said; —so I introduced her to Jack formally.

Through me, Jack told her he would fight for her rights just like I would and that she had great looking legs.

I tried to stop him, but demons are starved for any reality. Cindy hit me [and Jack] on the head and I apologized for him.

Then I told her she did look nice and Jack was only stating the obvious.

I started a stupid song and Cindy sang with me. She was a much better singer.

By the time we got to Tom's home, it was nighttime. We parked down the road and I asked Cindy to stay in the car for this first outing so we can make sure everything is good. I promised she would be able to witness some of his downfall.

Jack and I made easy access through the wall and found Tom asleep. Unfortunately, there was a woman with him.

I made a loud noise in the living room and Tom got up, took out his gun, and came downstairs. A frying pan flew from his kitchen and hit his wrist causing the gun to fire and fall on the floor. It floated up in the air and then vanished through the wall. Tom's visitor was yelling and getting dressed. She ran out of the house and Tom called the police.

Very quickly we were back in my car down the road and Cindy was a mess after hearing the gunshot.

I told her what happened and we waited for the police to come and go.

As soon as they were gone, we were back again. This time I brought Cindy and I explained what was going to happen. The three of us could not go through the wall so I had my soul enter her and Jack did the same. Let me tell you the first time someone invades your body is a shock, but when two entities sort of push their way into you and take over some of your being, it feels like dread, at first. Cindy slumped over, but I tried my best to comfort her in this odd situation. Soon, she had sort of made the transition and was ready to go.

All of a sudden, she grabbed her own boob. She yelled out, *"Who made me do that?"*

Jack came clean and apologized profusely and said he had never entered a woman's body like that and got a little excited and he promised on his life he would never do that again.

Cindy said, *"You'll have to do better than that. Your already dead."*

"You know what I mean", Jack said.

Actually, Cindy was doing all the talking and it must have seemed very strange. She said, *"Does he have to come along?"*

I told her, *"It would be safer just in case we need some extra strength or need to become invisible fast."*

She said, *"OK, but leave my hands alone."*

Together we went through the wall and floated to the bedroom. Cindy was just smiling and taking in the excitement almost as much as Jack.

Tom was trying to sleep, but he kept hearing a creaking sound from somewhere. His window opened and the bathroom sink and shower began spraying water. I had to really try to control Jack and Cindy's laughter as she was experiencing being invisible for the first time and Jack was experiencing being a woman.

Tom jumped out of bed and yelled for someone to stop. We did not listen. He looked in the mirror and I made his face look like a demon. He threw the mirror to the floor and went back to the phone to call the police. They took their time coming and we went to the kitchen and put a can of soup in his microwave and turned it on.

The explosion was glorious and horribly messy.

Tom actually began to cry, but he headed for his booze for some strength. As he drank. Cindy and I made him pour it all over himself. He smelled like a brewery as the cops came and we left for a while.

By this time, we were tired and we found a motel nearby and I was about to get two rooms when Cindy told me to only get one as she was kind of scared.

Don't get me wrong, there was no hanky-panky for several reasons. I was trying my best to be a gentleman; we were all too keyed up; and then there was Jack. He did make a suggestion for us to just forget he was there, but we knew his idea. Soon, we were all asleep and morning came.

Tom woke up to flat tires and he called the cops again. They found nothing and he was late for an important meeting. He hadn't even shaved.

He called off the meeting and headed for a bar. We went with him.

At the Bar, Cindy got a table in the back of the room as Jack and I became invisible again. We found a huge guy and whispered to him that Tom looked like someone he would like to know better. We already knew his inclination was for male partners and soon the man came over the Tom. We made the big guy think Tom had complimented his bottom and that Tom would like to sit with him. The big guy struck up a conversation, and we forced Tom to cross his leg. It was so funny to see him try to tell his new friend he wasn't doing that. I noticed the big guy slipped something in his drink and I found out it was not a harmful drug. Tom took some of his booze and began to get woozy. The big guy offered to take him home and the drunken Tom had little control about what was going on.

We went back to Cindy and we followed. While it would have been easier if Jack would have taken control of Tom at this time, he was way too afraid he would not have a chance at redemption so we simply followed. At the big guy's home, Tom was being carried up to the door as I left my body in the car and Jack and I took Cindy through the wall. By this time, Tom was starting to come around a little and the big guy introduced himself as Mike Long.

I made Tom say, "*You are handsome!*" and he tried his best to stifle his stupid mouth. He hit himself in the face and that didn't help.

Mike Long began taking off his clothes after that telling remark and Tom tried to run. Mike was not only long, he was fast and he caught Tom. Mike stated, *"You're pretty handsome yourself even if you play hard to get."* Tom's clothes were ripped away and Mike was ready for action as Tom was begging for anything and everything. Mike would not hear any of it and was almost to violate Cindy's molester, when she said, *"I think he has had enough."* As we floated above the scene, I made Cindy visible so that Tom would know he was being repaid.

Tom, yelled, *"Cindy! Help me,"* but Cindy had disappeared.

All of a sudden, one of Mike's frying pans came from his kitchen and bonked him on the head. It actually took 2 bonks to allow Tom enough time to run out into the street trying to get someone to notice him in his ripped tightie-whities, one arm in his shirt, and a sock halfway on and off.

Tom called for help, thinking the naked Mike was coming after him. Within a few seconds, Tom had regained his senses and ran out the door. For some reason Mike tripped in his lawn allowing Tom to run.

The police took the two lovebirds into custody until they could straighten out everything.

There was no doubt the papers would have a field day, but Tom would suffer for some time. ---- and we did it with almost no one getting hurt physically.

I wondered why a courtroom could not provide the same justice for Cindy, against those claiming respect in a community ignorant of truth.

Cindy actually felt sorry for her past rapist, for a minute, then we all went out for dinner.

Jack wanted something spicy.

After dinner, we all went back to Cindy's home. She could not stop thanking me and Jack.

She even made reference for us to stay the night. I thanked her for thinking of me, but that character needed to be taught a lesson before he did that to anyone else.

I said, *"He hurt one of my best friends in the whole world."* Jack made a grumbling sound but then he laughed or made me laugh--- I have a difficult time knowing what is visible and real all the time.

I asked her if we were still on for the weekend and she said, "Maybe, we can have a session tomorrow evening."

I kissed her lightly and told her to never fear so long as I was nearby. I would protect her with my life. Jack started to say the same goes for him, but he realized he was dead, so he kept quiet.

After my classes the next day, I went to get Cindy on what was really just a date rather than a session to discuss me being nuts. We had Italian and I left Jack back at home.

Cindy told me that I should take up some type of meditation program for my peculiar issues. She then indicated she had contacted a friend of hers who did what was called "Inspirational Yoga". I was already signed up to the class starting Saturday afternoon, right after our next session. I told her my body would not do the things they required and she assured me this was something entirely different. Then she said "How is your classroom demeanor?"

School

I told her, *"My classes were doing much better since I have started opening up."* I should have told someone long ago about what was going on, but Cindy was turning out to be my lifeline.

Anyway, I told her, *"We were discussing issues and concerns of the great worldwide flood at the end of the Pleistocene Age. I had made a handout for each of the students on Monday and it was now time for them to have open discussions. Most responded well to my suggestions concerning how God may have had a hand in destroying the people of the Pleistocene because of genetic manipulation similar to our current efforts, and for disbelief similar to our current understanding. Half the class was to take the high technology and religious deprivation side, while the other side was to be the counter group. Everything was going great and my students had pretty good, enlightened ideas on both sides. I could not be happier, but this same guy, Jake, began to belittle those who were assigned to go along with the narrative I had laid out."*

"You idiots!", he yelled, *"We are supposed to be learning about historical Anthropology and Mr. Manfred is a joke. His ideas have no factual basis and I, for one, am reporting his teaching to the University head."*

You would have been proud as I calmly told him, *"You don't have to stay in my class if you don't want to but don't try to limit the learning of the other students."*

"The others in my class clapped as the, less than reasonable, young man left to do his dirty work. I told the others to calm down and get back to work. I didn't raise my voice at all. It felt great to control my anger even when one of my students belittled my work, disrupted my class, and tried to get me fired. He was just misguided."

The student, Jake Jarvis, went to the Chancellor's Office and initiated another complaint.

"I must admit I brought Jack with me so that I could enter his locked car, change all the radio stations to Christian channels, move his front seat all the way up, flatten one of his tires, and put all his audio disks under his seat two days in a row. One of my students told me about his strangeness and that the police were tired of his rantings, he began to think his vehicle was haunted, he said he could even hear voices in his head, if you can imagine such a thing. One time he said his hand made a fist and hit his own head and another time he said his feet came off the ground and then he fell on his back. While he tried to tell others about what he believed to be truth, most believed he was a nutcase. I, on the other hand, believe we should understand that we should not judge what others have experienced or believe in. He never did come back to my class and my other students were glad."

Oh yes! The police discussed his oddness with the school officials so they did not take away my class.

Cindy said, *"Shame on you!"* I said, *"I didn't get mad!"* As you can imagine she came back with *"Don't you try to excuse your superman juvenile action."*—the only thing I really heard was you're a super man! Then she leaned over and put her head on me and softly said, *"I'm so glad you came to me for help. God has brought you to me. I even think Jack was brought to me by God."*

She didn't know the half of it, but there would be time to get her to see the big picture.

I told her good night and left her at her front door after giving her a pretty respectable kiss.

Trying to stay a compassionate gentleman, I said, *"Our next session will be at my house, don't you think?"* She said, *"That's great, but don't forget about the Yoga class."*

I made a weird face and said OK! Then I got in my car and went home.

Saturday

This session would be at my home. I tried to make something special, but I'm not a great cook. I asked Jake if he knew any recipes and he said something funny like lava cake and super fire chips. Then I said, never mind; I remember you burning down my kitchen. I think I'm making meatloaf. Jack said that isn't spicy but it tastes good. I made the stuff and potatoes and green beans and I was set for my session and sort of an intimate luncheon.

Dr. Cindy was at the door as I put the food in the oven. Not thinking, I asked Jack to get the door. He made me hit my own head.

I got to the door and took her coat as she came in with her computer ready. When I took her coat, I saw she was ready for Yoga. Yoga pants and the whole thing. I told her she looked nice. I did not tell her I had something planned for the session.

I finished getting lunch on and sat down to continue. I left off with the End of the Pleistocene in process and some are in vehicles to bring them to safety and my house was on fire.

"I went home for 3 days fighting a fire and all but I had a feeling I had to get back to Conrad and his band of survivors. Before I left I gave specific instructions to Jack and set him up with prepared foods. Then I grabbed the stone purse and I was back inside Conrad."

"We quickly acclimated and Conrad told me it had been 7 months since I left. The rain had stopped about 4 months ago and the only thing that could be seen was the top portions of mountainous regions. During that time the voyagers showed they would be able to help rebuild the Earth and they had probably been selected by God for this feat.

For the past 6 months, the vehicle had been in a fairly low orbit so the cinnabar fuel could be conserved and oxygen could be produced more easily. Martin and Tawni took the first watch as the remainder of the crew took Nestle-bane which slowed the heartrate and placed the crew in a sleep state. After the first month, Martin and Tawni went to sleep and Reese and Bonnie took their place. Now during the 6th month, Conrad and Maria were awake and another trip down close to the water showed the water to be like glass and tops of mountain were well above the waterline. Conrad decided to see if he could find Noah's floating hotel around the area he believed to be Turkey.

Meeting Noah

Thanks to the craftmanship of Reece the navigation system was now completely calibrated and it was determined that the Earth had truly shifted 32 degrees and now Turkey should be about 35 degrees north of the Equator. The vehicle knew where to go even if we didn't and soon, I could see we were over the Mediterranean Sea and unbelievably, we saw a tiny speck to the east. Noah's boat wasn't really a sailing craft as it was flat on the top and bottom and 3 or 4 heavy sea anchors would have been lowered as soon as the storms subsided to keep the hotel stable.

As we got close, we could see that a hole had been bored out near the top of the third story and the boat was riding very low with only the third floor above the waterline. Conrad set the dials for the vehicle to set down on top of the flat roof while he and Maria administered a "wake-up tonic" to those sleeping. The sleepy passengers got a shot by Conrad and soon everyone was awake and the vehicle had landed.

Within a few minutes a familiar face came through the hole and was on our landing area. Following Shem, was his pregnant wife. The hole was made larger and our crew made their way into a marvelous zoo. Each month, the animals were feed pellets of that nestle-bane herb and various food products so the animals never really were awake, except for chickens. Noah and the others were awakened and Conrad and Jamma gave each a nutrition shot to help them normalize faster. By this time everyone knew that I was back and that we had found the Ark of Noah. As normal Noah did most of the talking and told us about the horrors of the axis shift. The ark had flipped over 5 times during the roughest parts, but an angel was on board for a time to encourage Noah and his family. A fairly quick tour of the huge ship was very impressive and the chickens and little chicks followed us everywhere. After the worst of it, Noah's family had taken turns sleeping for a month or so at a time to conserve food and reduce boredom waiting for the boat to find its home.

Noah, blessed each of us, I filled them all in on my fire and life in the future and I told Noah he would have to wait another 5 months before the ship will dock according to various ancient texted. Japheth told about ½ dozen Ark jokes and we all laughed. Most weren't funny, but it was good to laugh. Then Bonnie took out her lyre and began singing a song about the flood. It went like this.

> *The flood drowned the world and all that was in it*
> *The sun came forth and died all our tears*
> *God and his angel protected us from harm*
> *Glory to the name or our Lord*

She must have sung 20 verses off the top of her head and soon everyone was trying to sing the song. I have to admit it, Bonnie was as close to being an angel as I have ever heard.

Jothan brought out some tiny sweet corn he had grown on the ship and Japheth fried eggs on a make shift grill. We had a feast. Jothan brought Noah a sack of various grains he had mixed that would provide a fast harvest for when they reached land and Noah gave us some chickens and chicks. It was like Christmas before there was a Christmas. We stayed for several hours and even helped feed the animals in the endless stalls. There was much kissing hugging and praying and then we were back in our own ship, rising into the air.

Cindy asked, *"Before you continue, can you tell me more about the people in this group. If you describe them to me, they may become more openly accessible to you and reduce stress whenever others don't believe what you know to be truth."*

Before we began, I provided her with a general lineage of the various people as I was pretty sure it was getting confusing.

Conrad's Family

The chart is shown next. I started with my direct connection with this time-space quantum thing. Conrad had 2 wives and now a daughter. He was a born leader. He was slightly larger than the others and his reddish complexion showed strength and resolve and his clean-shaven features sported a mustache. From my time with him, I understood his focus and his feeling that he was responsible for all those with him. It was he who first went to Noah to understand more of the ways of God and to get details of the impending doom. He had almost pushed his close family into joining him in his almost insane drive to get ready for the impending doom even before I came along.

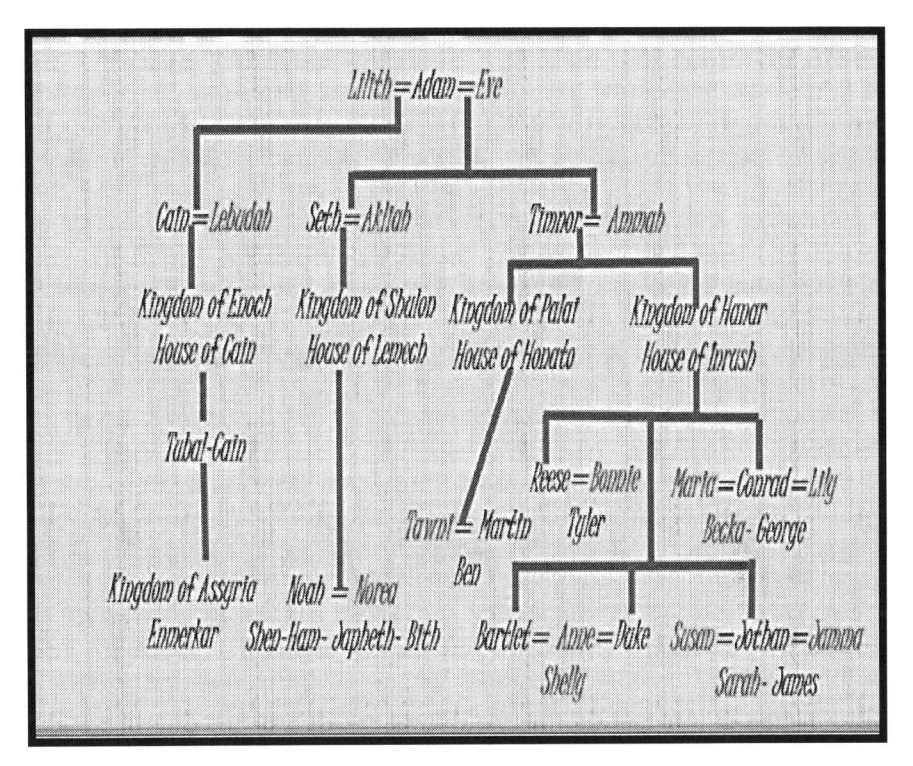

```
                    Lilith = Adam = Eve
         ┌─────────────┼──────────────┐
    Cain=Lebudah   Seth=Aklfah    Timnor=Amnah
         │              │               │
  Kingdom of Enoch  Kingdom of Shalon  Kingdom of Palai   Kingdom of Hanar
  House of Cain    House of Lemech   House of Honato    House of Thrush
         │                                                      │
     Tubal-Cain                                    ┌─────────────┤
         │                              Reese=Bonnie      Marla=Conrad=Lily
         │                       Tawni=Martin  Tyler       Becka- George
         │                              Ben         ┌──────────┴──────────┐
  Kingdom of Assyria  Noah=Norea                    │                     │
     Enmerkar      Shem-Ham-Japheth-Bith     Bartlet=Anne=Duke    Susan=Jothan=Jamma
                                                   Shelly           Sarah- James
```

It was Conrad's conviction that helped the others. I believe my visitations helped him gain the confidence he needed to lead and protect this important group of survivors, but he never wavered from his belief that it was his responsibility to get everyone to safety. Conrad had little fear of the unknown and welcomed a new beginning. When he was only 70 jubilee years old, that sounds funny just saying it. Anyway, he had suffered family lose to the Mystifiers of Palai, because of that, he was working on his distrust of Martin even with him having a wife who was of his own clan. Deep down he knew Martin was a good friend.

As a Biologic Engineer, Conrad had developed many new animals and helped to extend the quality of life of the other citizens with his investigations in life saving synthetic and biologic organ substitutes. His development of the toxic stomach virus and antidote also was critical to get Jothan out of the secured hospital and he had brought the "seed" of many animals" in the form of DNA sequences that would allow for the repopulation of a wide variety of animal types needed to support the populations. He also brought equipment needed to support implanting, recovery, inspection, regeneration and spicing of DNA to support all types of things including cures for disease.

<u>Maria, his first wife</u>- Maria was a horticulturalist who worked with Jothan. Her beauty was unmatched and, I think, it was her wisdom was what kept Conrad going forward in the right direction.

<u>Becka, Maria's Girl</u>-Whenever Maria got pregnant with her three-year-old girl, Becka, her focus was to make the world green again and to teach the others how to sustain it.

<u>Lily, his second wife</u>- Lily was the official librarian for the library of science. As such, she was the caretaker of the ancient knowledge and she assembled important works to take with them to insure details of science was not lost in the new world. She was probably the most outgoing and fun loving of the entire group. She was now pregnant with a boy who would be named George.

Jothan's Family

Jothan had 2 wives and a baby girl named Sarah. Jothan was a true scientist in Botany. He almost looked like Conrad's brother without the mustache. As with most of the Hanar clan he had a reddish complexion and he wore his hair similar to Conrad as he was more of an outdoor guy. He enjoyed camping so he would be in his element as the group finally tried to reestablish civilization from nothing and he showed strength and resolve.

From my time with him, I understood his love of nature, his free spirit, and his complete devotion to Conrad. He knew how dangerous his escape had been and how Conrad's drive had gotten them to where they were. While he did not have as strong a conviction about God, he knew God's hand was in their escape. I believe my visitations helped him bond more with those who were not as naturalistic.

As a Botanic Engineer, Jothan had been responsible in developing a large number of resistant strains of foods including resistances to drought, salty water. He also developed new quick flowering food types including a fast-growing grain similar to Wheat and a version of potato that absolutely could outgrow the fastest algae in the Ocean. He had lost a part of his left arm during his short stint in the Pleistocene Wars, but had a useful prosthetic which allowed him to have relatively good use of his arm and grasp things securely. Jothan brought a wide assortment of plant seeds and even small sprouted plants including his potato that he set up to provide sustaining food during the groups travels. His knowledge of what plants were edible and how to enrich soil to produce the best and fastest crops would greatly aid the rebuilding of civilization.

Jamma, his first wife- Jamma was a Doctor of veterinary studies who now was the group medic. She had already performed emergency surgeries and, eliminated all the embedded trackers, and had helped deliver babies. She would protect the group and bring into the new world the medicine of the Pleistocene.

James- Jamma's "soon to be" boy-Soon to be pregnant with a baby boy she named James, after me.

Susan, his second wife- Susan was the funniest of all the group and she was and would continue to be a teacher. Her specialty was in history, so she would carry the mantle of Science historian and teacher in this new world.

Sarah, Susan's baby girl-She had just had a baby girl named Sarah.

Reece's Family

Reece was a magnetics engineer. Reece had the Clan reddish complexion, but he had a smaller build and he wore longer hair including a well-trimmed beard. While he had never really gone camping and had a fear of the unknown, he trusted Conrad since he was 50 jubilee years old, when he had suffered similar family loses to those of Conrad to the Mystifiers. He was working on his distrust of Martin, but it was still a struggle. In his heart, he knew Martin was a good guy, that would forfeit his life for anyone of them but there had been so much death that still haunted him thousands of years after the destruction. He enjoyed tinkering and creating. He had designed special drones to aid in Jothan's escape and developed ways to make their vehicle almost invisible to the Magnetic radar systems. He had modified their weapons to make them fire farther by accelerating the projectiles with magnetic pulsing along the weapon barrel and he is the guy that actually got the abandoned aircraft up and running. The others helped, but it was his genius that figured out how to bypass and modify worn and damaged elements of the magnetic drive, navigation, and landing elements.

From my time with him, I understood his insecurities and how the friendship of Conrad and Bartley were so very important to him. While he loved all of the survivors, he struggled with a close relationship with Martin. He also had a strong love of God which made him slightly isolated as he wanted to spend time with the creator and he knew God had planned all of the steps needed in their escape including my visitation.

You could say Reese was the brains of the group. As a Magnetics Engineer, Reese had been responsible for developing a wide variety of interplanetary drive systems using Cinnabar and magneto-lux engine designs adopted from the early Anak models. He designed ways to establish earth resonance to allow for more efficient electrical distribution from the Egyptian source engine, and also had designed weapons to be used in the long-lasting Pleistocene wars. Reese brought all type of schematics, components and weapons he had designed As a Magnetics Engineer, Reese had been responsible for developing the infrastructural energy distribution methods of two different municipalities and he understood how the group could tap into the energy emanating from the massive Pyramidal Electrical generator developed by the great King Thoth of Egypt. He also understood how we could establish remote energy from the variations of the magnetic field established by solar wind hitting Earth's atmosphere and the continuous bombardment of neutrinos from the sun. Just to let you know how deep into this stuff he studied, his College Thesis was on "Neutrino Capture and the Integration of Mercuric gas from Cinnabar", so, he was pretty much a genius when it came to building all types of engines for transporters, weapons, and construction tools. Later, many of his inventions would be used by the Egyptian and PreIncan societies to construct massive and intricate structures that would save many lives.

<u>Bonnie- His wife</u>- Bonnie, was the main musician and singer at a local restaurant as such she would be able to bring the travelers joy as they fought fear and danger. She was very talented and knew how to play what they called a lyrette, a cross between a lyre and a 2-string base instrument. Besides playing the lyre, the instrument would keep beat by playing one string then the other and the musician would move a slider to change the pitch of the base backup. It was a neat instrument for sure.

I made a sketch of this instrument, but I have no record of this type of instrument found anywhere.

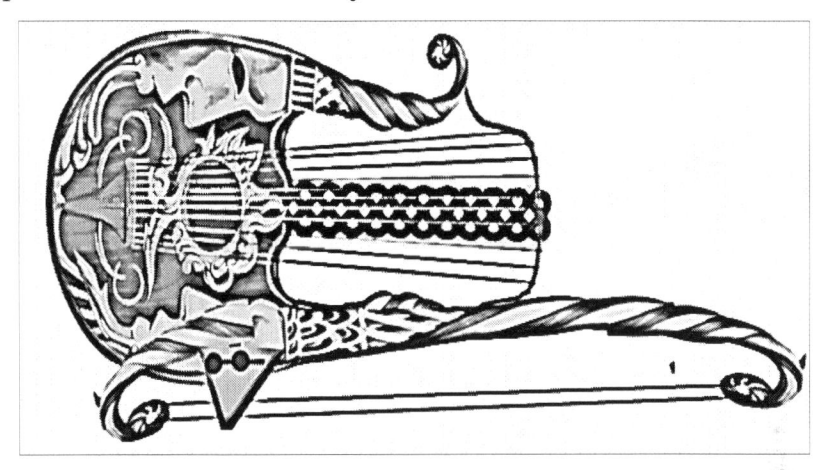

Tyler, her boy-Whenever she got pregnant with her three-year-old boy, Tyler, her focus was to teach him and the other children how to make the world great through music and how to advance the teachings of God. She always thought the father of little Tyler was "partially" me and reminded me all the time. Bonnie would become the musician of a new civilization.

Bartlet's Family

Bartlet was a commercial pilot and mechanic. Bartlet had reddish complexion and a medium build and he wore his hair short with a close-cut mustache. He was the youngest of the men at only 400 jubilee years old only to be unseated by Anne who was only slightly younger. Bartlet had no fear of the unknown, he trusted Conrad since he was a few hundred years old, when his first wife was killed during the war. Because Conrad vouched for Martin, he knew Martin was a good guy. He enjoyed any kind of flying, working with machinery, and engines. He and Reece did almost all the rebuilding of the flying ship they escaped on. From my time with him, I understood his insecurities and how the friendship of Conrad and Bartlet were so very important to him. While he loved all of the survivors, he struggled with a close relationship with Martin. He also had a strong love of God much like Reece and he knew God had planned all of the steps needed in their escape including my visitation.

As a commercial pilot and mechanic, Bartlet had been responsible for the update of a transport fleet for the university and he had been their principle pilot. He also had supported the war as a transport pilot, but never had to be directly involved. His knowledge of machines proved invaluable when trying to repair the old flying machine and his almost fearless capabilities as a pilot had already allowed the escape of some of the team. Bartlet's first wife had died many years ago, but Anne, who was wife to both Bartlet and Duke had been a great wife and mother to "their" son Shepard.

Anne, Bartlet's second Wife-—Anne was a physical therapist of sorts and held exercise training in a small gym she ran with a friend named Karen. She was totally fit and never ate meat. While this seems strange to me, one could tell it did not he hurt her. She was the most physically fit of the group and she encouraged the group to take part in her daily exercise routine. She would also teach all the children how to live healthy. Now pregnant, she would have a girl named Shelly. Generally speaking the exercises she used were similar to those we use today. I guess, working muscles always needs movement of the muscles about the same way.

Shephard [son of Anne and Duke or Bartlet]- Shephard had been a Supervisor for a war supply house and a good one, but his number came up and he was drafted into the Army only to be pulled out by his Mom, Dad, and Conrad.

Duke 2nd Husband of Anne- Duke had the same light complexion and reddish hair, but he wore his hair a little longer than the others down the back and he wore a beard and mustache similar to Reese. He was the "other" husband of Anne and he, sort of, got mixed up in this accidentally, however he became a true believer after a time and he loved Bartlet, Anne, and Shephard; and would come to love all the others in the group as a family. As a city planner and contractor, Duke was great with his hands including, Carpentry, Building, Plumbing, Electrical installation, City Planning, and just about anything structural. After Bartlet focused on preparing for the end of the Pleistocene, Duke took care of Anne and Shephard who may have been Duke's or Bartlet's son. After saving Shepard from the military, he joined the group to do whatever he could. His knowledge of construction would be greatly appreciated in the new land with almost no surviving structures.

Martin's Family

Martin was a Chemist, Mystifier, and Army Guard who was now wanted for treason in a land that had disappeared. Unlike the others, Martin and his family were from the Palai clan. Because the Mystifier Army of Palai had destroyed the capitol city of Hanar, he and his family, along with all the rest of the Palai-ites, were hated by the people of Hanar. Like the other Palai clansmen, he had a somewhat brown complexion and dark brown hair, he was tall and thin in build, and he wore short hair with a finely manicured mustache. He was a true outsider, but he had befriended and aided in the escape of Jothan. Martin was an avid camper and knew how to survive in the wilderness better than the others. He had almost no fear of the unknown, he trusted Jothan implicitly from my time with him, I understood his insecurities and how the friendship of Conrad and Bartlet were so very important to him. As a chemist, it was up to him to make the herbs and treatments suggested by Jamma, Conrad, and Jothan into forms that could be ingested and he would also find new chemical combinations to produce high enough electronegativities to establish better batteries. It actually was Martin that developed the first Lithium-Manganese battery, but his combination was lost though time. As the avid camper, he would train the group, who were now on an extremely long camping trip, how to survive. It would be found that having the capability to repel down the side of a mountain would be important when they realized they were over a thousand feet in the air after the water receded sufficiently. As a Mystifier, his capability to disappear and to levitate objects had already been useful and it would certainly be needed for their survival to come.

Tawni his only wife-- "Tawni was the artist of the group. There cannot be enough said about how art affects our modern societies and it would be the same with Tawni. She possibly was the first to understand how to make motion pictures by drawing sequences of images in order and spinning the pot or whatever that held the, now animated event. I believe, it was one of her creations that actually survived the ravages of time." Tawni was not of Palai, but instead, was of the Hanar Clan like Conrad, although I was not sure the exact heritage.

I showed Cindy the only known surviving motion picture machine from around 7 to 9 thousand years ago. It was found in the area now known as Pakistan, today, but Tawni would make these things all the time. The one I showed her has an antelope jumping to eat from tall grass that can be seen by spinning the 'image base' and blinking at the appropriate speed. She made one of a man climbing a mountain. I'll never know if Tawni made the ancient movie shown next, but it gives you an idea of her creativity.

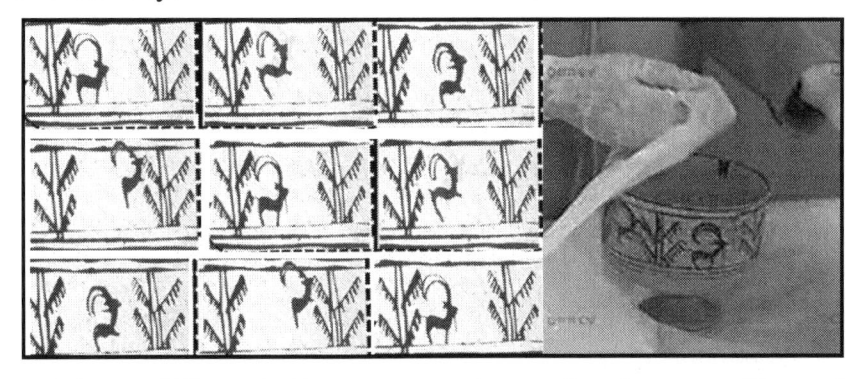

Ben, Son of Tawni- Ben was an Agent for the war effort who later was drafted into the war. After our rescue, he had proved to be a skilled fighter. With the weapons designed by Reece, Ben could hit objects at almost twice the distance of the others. OK! Ben was at least a couple thousand years younger, so his eyes might have been sharper, but I never really found out how old he really was. It would be Ben that saved the group when confronted by starving people who would do anything to survive.

The Group

"That was the crew of the new Conradian Colony who would reestablish a new world order. They would have to fight to ensure they survived as wayward survivors of the floods were now almost dying of starvation and they would do anything to survive."

A general sketch of the team is shown below so Cindy could put a face to the various names.

With that little bit of background, Cindy, and I hope you have a clearer understanding of who the group and how they somehow had the needed capabilities to build a strong community. I don't know if this was accidental or divine providence, but I found that Conradia, the contested name of the surviving kingdom would last for well over a thousand years after the Flooding had ended. First they had to find land.

190

Finding Land

After leaving Noah, the group never left a low flightpath so they could examine potential landing sites. They had been systematically landing on those areas that could serve as take-off platforms, but they had not found a reasonable long-term landing platform nor had they seen any other vehicles. Something told me this would be the day and that is why I had been returned to this time. Shepard was at the pilot seat. He had become a pretty good pilot. The crew had decided that half would sleep while the other half would be awake and on the lookout for survivors and; more importantly, survivors who would attempt take control of our ship to target food. From the start, the survivors had been on food rations as there were more survivors than they originally had determined. As far as new situations, Lily was now pregnant and so was Bartlet's wife Anne, but the best news was that Susan, Jothan's wife, now had a baby girl. The 17 survivors were running low on supplies but they knew others would have the same issue. Collectively, they had 14 weapons and a mysterious box brought by Martin. Three of the weapons were high powered and the others were hand weapons or close quarters sub machine guns.

Off the port side, I mean left, Ben saw a flat area on the lower part of a mountainous region. Not only was the area relatively flat, but it also had a small patch of green on the ground. Reece had tried to recalibrate their navigation equipment after the entire Earth axis shifted and it indicated they were somewhere near the Caspian Sea, give or take a thousand miles, but they decided to land and check out the area. Not far from the clearing they found a small cavern that could be used for protection so they transferred their remaining stores and hid the entrance as best they could. As it turned out the green areas contained edible grasses so the team built a fire, made a soup and all ate from the first harvest in this new land.

Unbelievably, it wasn't an hour after eating that another ship was noticed on the horizon. The chances this land would not be seen was very low, so the team gathered whatever they could and headed for the cavern. In this new land, they would have to fight for survival.

Luckily, the ship passed on the other side of the mountainous region and did not spot the landing area of the indications of life and they flew into the sunset. While they had praised God for deliverance while on the ship, they all got together to praise God again for protecting them and showing them this land.

Oh Well!

As darkness came upon us, both Martin and Jothan came to Conrad to request a sexual adjoining as Jamma and Tawni were still hoping they could also bring a new life into this new land and they all believed, my manipulation of DNA somehow allowed for their mutual satisfaction and productivity. Conrad excused himself from Maria and Lily who had linked up with Jothan and Conrad initiated a different party of sorts in this small plot of land. While I still could not get used to the freedom of lovemaking in this ancient society, it would be this strong bonding and love between the Hanar clan that would allow it to thrive, and it had now added the new group of Palai-ites. There were other spontaneous exchanges going on while Conrad was busy ensuring all the women could be reinvigorated with the capability of reproduction that was believed to come from my adjoining. I really could not complain as these people really meant business when it came to trying to satisfy others they cared for. Conrad would sleep well tonight.

Bartlet stood guard, most of the night and he was relieved by Reece as dawn broke. What he saw sent shivers down his spine as he woke the others and a ship was landing near the location of their somewhat hidden ship. Luckily the weapons and Martin's mysterious box had been unloaded and added to the articles in the cave early the day before.

Time to Eat and Yoga

With that little bit of detail, I stopped describing the past and concentrated on our food. The meatloaf was finished and we ate some good food. OK! It was good considering I made it. The meatloaf was an old family secret recipe. One box of cornflakes, hamburger meat, ½ a small bottle of ketchup, some chili sauce, an egg, and a little seasoning. The stuff was smashed into a loaf and cooked. Surprisingly, it tasted really good.

Cindy indicated she liked it a lot and even Jack said he could taste a little zing. After eating, Cindy helped me with the dishes and I left to get ready for out Inspirational-Yoga appointment.

To be funny, I found some leotard-type pants and a muscle shirt. Then I finished off scene with a ballet-type-tutu-skirt.

I came out and was ready to go back to the bedroom to put on regular clothes, but, unfortunately, she said, *"-------perfect!"*---------?????????

We arrived in the park just as the instructor friend arrived. Jack came along to laugh into my head.

I curtsied and said *"How do you do?"* to my new instructor. She was wearing about the same thing as Cindy, but when she saw me she said, *"Perfect."*

Her name was Claudia, and I grabbed her arm to find out was I was in for. Best I can say is she was a holdover of the flower-people revolution of the '60s. I helped her with mats and soon another couple came to the location. The man was wearing jeans. I'll bet he felt out of place!!

Soon, light music was on and the entire class [three couples] were ready. She showed us the first torturous pose and I did as well as the other two guys, but then she said that we had to hold the pose until our partner was satisfied with an answer to a question, she randomly pulled out of a bowl.

The women were first. The other couple Jim and Sally were ready. Sally asked, *"When was the last time you told me you love me?* Jim said, *"Day before yesterday."* She came back with. *"Why not today?"* He said' *"I love you,"* then he was allowed to release the pose. The second couple Frank and Alice said almost the same things and Frank did not have to hold his pose long.

This possibly wouldn't be so bad. That tutu thing was hiding my almost exposed manliness pretty well, but I had already been holding this pose for the first 2 questions, now I had more.

As Cindy asked me when I told her I loved her and I said, *"I love you if you let me down."* The others laughed and I released my torture.

The next question was a little less intimate as it was, *"When did I make dinner for you and what was it?"* This was asked by the men and Cindy and Sally answered easily, but Alice said, Frank never made her anything, which was wrong, then she remembered peanut butter sandwich and was allowed to release her torture.

The next one was a bad one. *"Tell me how many people you had had sex with and their names."*

The first two guys said their women friends were there first. Then it was my turn. Cindy said, *"Tell me how many people you had had sex with and their names."* This was going to be embarrassing.

I said, "About 14- mostly women, but also with 3 men and one dead guy---sort of". I tried to stay focused, but the other couple and the instructor stopped everything and came closer to hear what I was going to stay. Jim whispered the word freak to his partner.

My first encounter was in college to a girl named Gwen. I was so excited, I finished before I started and Gwen laughed. I didn't go out with her again, nor did I do much dating.

My next encounter was with a man named Conrad, his two wives Marian and Lily, and their neighbor, Bonnie. This lasted for about 4 hours.

My next encounter was with—I looked around and everyone was looking at me and my tutu as my stupid foot was over my head. How embarrassing. My next encounter was with 2 girls, Susan and Lily, as well as Conrad.

The next encounter was with a girl named Anne and Conrad. This event took less than 2 hours.

The next encounter was with two girls and two guys; Tawni, Jamma, Martin, Jothan. Jim yelled out, "How long was that event?" and his partner hit him on the head. I said, "It took about 4 hours and I think I was really tired."

The last encounter was with a girl and a dead guy, but I don't really want to go into that.

Now I had to wait for Cindy to say OK. She said, *"You could have left out the dead guy."* Luckily, she said the answer was good before I ripped my Tutu. As I fell on the ground, my whole side cramped up.

Just about the time my cramp was easing a little, it was the guys turn. And another twisty body pose. Frank asked, *"What type of man are you attracted to?"* Alice said, *"you silly."*

Jim asked the same question and Sally quickly came back with, *"I'm not sure yet, "But I think those who are not ashamed to wear tutus and sleep with dead guys sound interesting!"* Jim said, *"Just how long do you want to stay in that Yoga pose anyway?"* OK! She reported, *"you are the man I adore!"* and Sally was released from agony.

Cindy's answer was, *"I used to like men with weird ears."* I laughed and she was released.

The Girl's question was, *"What do you like about my body?"* The answers were as expected. My answer was--- *"The whole thing- inside and out."*

Now it was the guys turn to ask and my turn. I said, *"What did you do to your last boyfriend?"*

- Cindy laughed and said, *I cried for a couple of months because of how horribly he had treated me.*
- *Then I found out where he was living, had some friends make him think he saw a ghost; then knocked his gun out of his hand as it went off; and stole the weapon. The police were called, but my friends could not be found.*
- *When they left, he was hit by a frypan and his tires mysteriously went flat.*
- *Then I had a dead guy and another guy get inside me.*
- *With the two of them attached I, somehow, followed him to a Bar.*
- *My friends convinced a massive homosexual guy, who went by the name Mr. Long, that my ex thought he, the homosexual mountain, was sexy. He made a gesture; my 'ex' could not disregard so the gay man took him home with him as my friends and I followed.*
- *My 2 friends and I were still attached but somehow able to get inside the guys house as he was preoccupied. There were clothes being ripped off, some screaming, and quite a bit of terror.*
- *My 'ex' saw me for an instant, but I was quickly hiding again and did not help him as he pleaded.*
- *From out of nowhere, a frypan hit the attacker and my 'ex' ran out screaming as he tried to pull up a portion of his underwear.*

- *Both my 'Ex' and the gay man were arrested and many people took pictures of the scene.*
- *Since his release, it is believed, others are not sure what type of person he really is.*

I said, "*Good enough,*" and she released he pose. Jim, Sally and Claudia were all clapping as she finished. I was proud that she was able to say all of that and clapped as well.

Unfortunately, for Claudia's class, we sort of messed up the ambiance. Frank and Alice just said that is just too much for us. We tried to do a couple more things, but Jim and Sally would just start laughing and saying something like – "*I had a dead guy inside me*" or, "*I was sleeping with 2 men and 2 women at the same time*", and burst out laughing.

We laughed along with them and could not hold a pose so we did a couple more twisty things and the class was called on account of laughter. Claudia said she had never heard anything like what we had said and there was no doubt we were made for each other, except for maybe the dead guy sex stuff.

Just to stoke the fire, Cindy, said, "*The dead guy is named Jack. He's harmless and I like him.*"

Claudia just shook her head, turned around and left us at our getaway car. I said, "*This tutu thing is pretty sexy isn't it?*" Cindy said, "*No!*"

We went back to my home, and Jack, Cindy, and I had a nice cup of coffee, before Cindy had to go. Jack kept bugging me about how the Tutu went over. I told him, everyone said it was the right outfit.

Jack said, "*I should have gone.*"

I kissed Cindy and she said goodnight and began to leave after making a next session the next weekend.

As she was going she said, *"I think it was better that Jack did not go."*

'Jack said, *"I heard what you said. Are you still mad at me for grabbing you when we possessed you?"*

Cindy said, *"No, but if it ever happens again, James will have a one-armed demon."*

I'm not sure what she meant by that, but Jack apologized again.

Visitors

I had a great time in my classroom, but I was certainly glad when Saturday came along. I met her at her home, she made brunch, and told me the crazy Saturday Yoga was a lot of fun. She asked if I wanted to do it again. I said, *NO!"*—She agreed, *"I'm not sure others are ready for us right now."*

After a couple of sips of coffee, she was at her computer and I was sitting across from her ready to continue. I left off before we found out about our unwelcome guests.

Back on the Mountain

"Martin became invisible and scouted the area. When he returned he filled the others in on the bad news. This was a group of about 10 people who were well armed and seemed to be very hungry. They pulled up much of the remaining grass and ate it so fast they didn't even notice the other ship not a hundred yards from their campsite. This time, Conrad went out to see what could be done. Our immediate task was to remove their weapons. We went in invisibly and I was his eyes. We quickly got to their ship and we were able to remove a large cash of their weapons.

To leave with the weapons, we floated over their heads and we were not noticed. With these weapons we stood a reasonable chance at taking control and we had the advantage of quantity, but many of our people were children or pregnant women.

Confrontation

Once we had all the weapons we could see, Conrad decided that an envoy should describe why the visitors could not stay on this fragile land. The emissaries would be Conrad [and me]; along with Jothan and Martin, who had just spent time in the military. We came with our own weapons and when we reached their camp, they seemed to surrender very quickly.

The group was made up of 2 Anak and, from the Clan of Cain, 4 men and 4 women. It was certainly apparent the Anak had control of the group and from their distress in getting food, we could tell they had not stored enough to eat for the trip. Without letting them know what was happening, Conrad held onto each while the other 2 secured the rest of the area as best they could. The Cainites were more afraid of the Anak than the all of us with weapons. When Conrad got to the Anak, he found out why. There had been 14 humans aboard the escape ship originally, but without food, the Giant Anak soon became so hungry they periodically killed one of the lesser ones. The killings had been done by a lottery. At one point one of the women had to eat a portion of her own husband.

It was the second Anak that gave me the most dreadful details and he was one called a "varactor". I found out Varactors, similar to Mystifiers, could produce an electromagnetic beam from their hand, but many times more powerful. They could also establish a force field around an area. I would find out that all early Anak could make this electromagnetic force field. One made a field around both of the giants while the other made a force field around the entire group. I knew Conrad and Martin could become invisible and make their way through the force field to safety, but Jothan would soon be killed so we had to come up with another plan. The first plan was to hide behind the Cainites, but after two were simply removed, we each hid behind different protrusions on the ground. I quickly became invisible and came up behind the Anak. Martin became invisible, but he was blind when invisible so he moved very little. This would not last as electromagnetic laser blasts were being fired. Another Cainite was blasted and we, certainly, would follow.

All of a sudden, the outside force field was being drained and the Cainites and Jothan quickly escaped the grip of the Anak. Conrad had made it through the second forcefield, but confrontation with the Anak was an impossible feat alone. The second field was now being drained just like the other one and the effect was devastating to the Anak. Jothan aimed and hit his mark, a small area in the neck of Anak was the weakest area. The second one escaped to the flying craft and he was able to escape without his food.

We were certain God would have his way with the Anak but what was the group going to do with 5 Cainites that were still alive after the very short, but dangerous battle and Martin had some explaining to do.

Conrad knew when it was firing, it was the *"Sword of Light"* of Leboa the Palai-Mystifier. Leboa was responsible for the death and enslavement of many of the people of Hanar. Martin was now having to explain that Leboa was his great-aunt and the accursed weapon had been passed to him on her death as he was entering the military and it was thought it could protect him. I reread the portion of the sacred book *"Generations of Adam"* to Cindy, so she would understand what had happened.

"Generations of Adam"- *The people of Palai were expert in many devices, and there was one among them, <u>Leboa, who devised a **sword of light [Light-Saber]**, which penetrated the wall of defense [force field] around the City of Haner and began to drain the power from the wall.</u>*

Ben had operated the ancient weapon and everyone came over to thank his quick actions and bravery. Then we thanked God for our escape before looking back at the Cainites.

What are we going to do? They all questioned.

Cainites

The term Cainite really had no meaning anymore. Neanderthal, Denisovan, and other humans who had been modified by Anak from the original Homo-Erectus human created by God had all been inbred with the descendants of Cain, those who had left the plateau of Adam, and the Anak. There was no way of really knowing heritage without DNA sampling and Conrad was not about to even worry about it.

Right now, these people needed food and companionship outside the Anak monster who was eating them.

There were 2 males and 3 females who survived the last slaughter.

After giving them food and proper clothing, we all introduced ourselves and let them understand they could stay. I had already touched each one, and knew they would not be harmful to the group. Additionally, I did what I could to reduce a huge amount of trauma they had suffered. When I knew, Conrad knew as well.

Bambie-The first girl to speak was named Bambie [like the deer]. She was sort of married to Mombo. They had a small boy, who had been eaten in front of them soon after the flooding began. Bambie was a physicist of sorts and a mechanical engineer by trade.

Mombo- Her quasi-husband went next. He was sort of an industrial Engineer and had headed up a manufacturing plant building radios before the end came to their worlds.

Both thought ZaZam and Barron, the two Anak, were gods and they were working in ZaZam's business when the possibility of disaster came and the Planet Venus died. By the time they realized they were evil people, it was too late.

Sadie- The second girl went next and introduced herself as Sadie. I was truly shocked that Cainites knew the language of Hanar, but many things shocked me about what I experienced. Her husband was one of those who had been killed in our initial meeting and she had lost a daughter as food for those who were certainly less than gods. Oddly, Sadie had been a reporter and had been reporting the horrible event at the end of the Pleistocene. Bartlet had even remembered seeing one of her broadcasts. She was also a meteorologist, so she certainly was not popular during the end days.

Carla- The next girl, was substantially younger, possibly about the same age as Ben. She told the group her name was Carla and that both her parents had been on the trip and were both gone. She began to cry. Bambie and Lily, quickly came over and hugged her. She told the others that she was in construction when the world ended.

Shawn- If there was a leader of this tattered group it was Shawn. He was in the military and had been home visiting Bambie and Mombo when his life was swept away by the floods. He was not eaten because he was the strongest of the group and apparently his gods had wanted him for breeding and, ultimately, slavery.

Without exception they asked who we had prayed to and Conrad filled in a century of missed understanding by this small group. They praised this new God for saving them and after the shock had finally settled down, with a little help from a shot provided by Jamma, they all began to cry like babies. The others comforted them as I left to ensure my home was still standing. Conrad kissed Maria and Lily so I could say bye and I went back to my "normal" body.

Did I say normal?????

I showed Cindy a graphic indicating the 2 types of people called out in Judeo-Christian were Jew and Gentile. Jews were pure Cro-Magnon and there are none alive today. Everyone else, including the Anak and half-breed Cro-Magnon and earlier human hybrids, are called Gentile. Most of these people died before or during the Extinction.

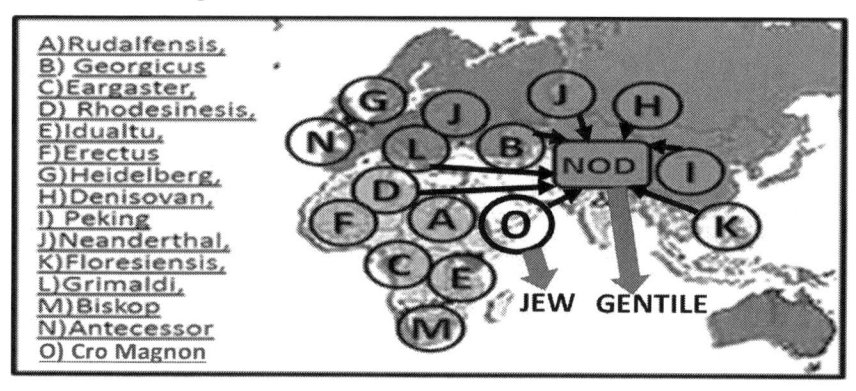

A) Rudalfensis,
B) Georgicus
C) Eargaster,
D) Rhodesinesis,
E) Idualtu,
F) Erectus
G) Heidelberg,
H) Denisovan,
I) Peking
J) Neanderthal,
K) Floresiensis,
L) Grimaldi,
M) Biskop
N) Antecessor
O) Cro Magnon

JEW GENTILE

I told Cindy the Gentile melting pot had just gotten larger and we decided to go eat.

Restaurant

After my session, Cindy and I went to a nice restaurant. The food was great and the company was even better. Things seemed like they were progressing with doctor and me, beyond friendship; but I didn't want to push it too hard as most of my earlier relationships---OK! All of my earlier relationships did not work out due to my substantial baggage.

Jack was in my head and said, "*Get something spicy*".

I ordered the prime rib and a salad. Cindy said that sounds good for me as well.

During our meal, Cindy told me how very much she appreciated how I had made Tom sense the same shame and fear that he had caused her; how much she enjoyed the silliness of that Yoga class; and very much she enjoyed being with me. She also told me about a troubled boy she was treating.

I know the whole confidentiality mess, but what can I say, I'm nosey and asked her what's wrong?

She told me the boy was a senior in High School but he was slightly smaller than others in his class. To make it worse, he was in the band. He was being bullied and she was struggling concerning how to go forward with him. If she had not experienced the relief from the Tom incident, she thought she would tell him to ignore the ridicule, but now she wasn't sure.

To make me bite, I think, she added, the boy's name is James and he loves ancient history. [Can you see the fish-hook?]

She explained that almost every day, two or more of the football players would catch him during his last class, Gym, and torment him. She was afraid of the damage that was being done.

I asked, *"What would you think would help?"*

Do you think we could influence the others so that they would want to leave him alone?

You guessed it, we were going to his school Monday.

I made arrangements for substitution again and we were ready to save the world again. One step at a time.

Monday

I, actually, started fairly soon after James arrived. Cindy pointed him out and I went with him to each class. The guy did like ancient history and he was a great clarinetist, but maybe those were part of the problem. He, certainly, was a shy one. I needed to boost his confidence.

In his first class, History, James' teacher asked him to tell the class something about the 15th dynasty of ancient Egypt. For a second it looked like he was going to simply say, he wasn't sure, like he always did but this time as if an answer was given to him he said, *"While the 15th dynasty is generally known as the Hyksos, Shepherd Dynasty", new research has determined that an invasion of Amalekites infiltrated Egypt and took control away from the 14th, 16th, and 17th Dynasties to reign supreme over almost all of Egypt for 150 years from 1700 to 1560BC. It would be this group that forced the Jews into bondage and the last major king of this dynasty, King Apepi, who would be drowned in the Red Sea as the Jewish Exodus would be the end of this oppressive Dynasty."*

The teacher was in shock and said, *"I'm going to have to read up on that great insight. Thanks, James"*

James was pretty much in shock himself, but he kept it together. The rest of the students wondered how he knew all that stuff. After class, one of his classmates, named Janis, came up to him and told him he really made the class interesting for a minute or two.

Then she said, *"See you in Band class."* As it turned out she also was a clarinetist and in his class.

As the day went on, Band class had Janis, coming to him and asking if they could study and practice together sometime. James said, *"That would be fine with me."*

She said, *"How about tomorrow afternoon? I could come over to you house if you like."* He told her where he lived and Janis gave him her phone number.

Then came the dreaded Gym class. This day they were playing baseball and when it was his turn to bat, hit a high fly-ball, but for some reason, no one caught it. Once they got the ball and threw it, no-one caught the ball, and James was now on third base.

The next batter hit a grounder and was heading to first base and somehow James ran faster than he normally did and the ball was thrown to home and the catcher missed as James slide in for the last run of the day.

The football heroes came over to suggest his luck was not going to last long today.

Out of his mouth came, *"I think my skill will continue for a while and leave me alone."*

The bully said, *"You can't talk to me that way punk!"* and he grabbed James' arm which somehow made the bully fall flat on his face. When he finally got up, his face was full of dirt and James somehow said, *"Don't call me punk!"*

A friend of dirt face told James he would be in trouble after school and dirt face added his threat.

At this point James was scared to death and I had to let him in on what was going on. He was almost as scared about the revelation as he was of getting beaten up.

I explained that he could not be hurt today so he simply needed to address the hoodlums in a friendly but forceful manner and I would do the rest.

After school just outside the schoolyard, there football players were waiting for James. As I instructed, he was polite to them. A group had formed around what they believed to be a massacre.

One guy grabbed James from the back and a second was coming in for a blast, but James dropped to one knee and the punch connected with the guy behind James. James somehow rose to his feet so fast, that a third assaulter, who was trying to kick him lost his balance and James fell on top of his face just as the kicker's foot made contact with the 2nd guy's knee.

A yell was heard and the second player moved out of the fight and the guy in the back got mad at the kicker and kicked him in the groin. He was also out and yelling.

This left one more bully. He was ready to plumule James in the face his first swing was a miss as James jumped away and the second one reached air as well. James calmly asked him to stop this hostility, but he made another attempt. James grabbed the attacker's fist in both hands and threw him to the ground. And then James told him to please stop before someone gets hurt! The football student said, *"OK!"*, and James reached out his hand to help him up and not embarrass him anymore.

Then he went over to the others and asked if they were ok and that he was very sorry for what he had done to them. His humility in his win affected the bullies. Then he asked if they were ok at calling this a draw and forgetting anything happened. He reached out his hand and the guy who was dead-set on kicking him allowed him to help him up. The groin-hit guy would take a minute.

The whole thing took less than 5 minutes, but it appeared the boys would not pick on him again and they might even be tolerant of him as a real person. All this, and no one was seriously harmed.

Cindy was in the crowd watching from the rear.

I checked on James' feelings and he seemed to be much less timid after this one event. I had a good feeling that he had made a step towards the confidence he needed. His hate for the boys was completely gone and now he was going to play clarinet with Janis.

At my car, I became visible and Cindy hugged me and Jack. She even thanked Jack for helping but I got a kiss. OK! Jack also got a kiss, but it was meant for me.

Our next visit would be Saturday again.

Calm Before the Storm

We again met at Cindy's home and she did not set up another Yoga thing. After a quick brunch. We sat at our USUAL places and I began again.

Back to the Survivors

"It would be about 4 days before I could get back to the group. What I found was good and bad. For the Hanar-ites, it had been a little over 4 years.

Conrad was troubled. The Cainites had integrated with the others very well and were studying the details of righteousness set down by the great Enoch. The whole group had now moved from the high plateau they had been on and now were in a beautiful valley and the community had expanded to 34 individuals. Shawn became Bambie's second husband, Sadie became Martin's second wife, and Ben had married Carla; and there were quite a few children.

They had left the small area that ended up high on the side of a mountain and had settled in a beautiful meadow filled with blossoms and a stream that rant through the village. It was connected to a large river not too far away. It was a great place to build a society, so you can imagine, the survivors would have to fight to keep it.

Duke and Carla, and basically designed and build the entire town and the river was used to provide electricity for the rag-tag society. They also, were now constructing a wall for protection. Shawn was helping by describing and building different elements of protection he learned in his military career.

Conrad, and Martin set up a lab for experimentations in biology and chemistry. Conrad had modified some captured birds so that they could not fly and produced twice as many eggs. Half were eaten and the others were used for stock. Now the community had plenty of meat. Martin had designed a filtration system that could eliminate almost all harmful chemicals in the water, and the refuse was modified as fertilization elements to build crops. Martin also built a chemical weapon that would temporarily blind invaders that could be used almost like Conrad's, stomach virus. When they were experimenting, the duo was building protection into the community including a tunnel safety system.

Susan and Lily were busy detailing the history and science that was being made and teaching the little ones. They also were tasked at babysitting the little ones; all 15 of them. Luckily, Becka, Tyler, George, and Sammy helped a lot. Not only were they taught about the great knowledge from the Pleistocene, but also how to protect themselves in nature and in war.

- Maria's girl Becka [10 years old]
- Bonnie's boy-Tyler [10 years old
- Lily's boy George [8 years old]
- Anne's boy Sammy [8 years old]

- Susan's girl Sarah [6 years old]
- Jamma's boy James [6 years old]
- Maria's boy Jackson [5 years old]
- Bambie & Mombo' boy Mike [4 years old]
- Bonnie's 2nd girl- [Sasha 3 years old]
- Jamma's girl Joy- [Joy 3 years old]
- Sadie's girl Shelly [2 years old]
- Lilly's 2nd boy Joe [2 years old]
- Carla's boy Bobby [1-year-old]
- Susan's 2nd girl Sadie [1-year-old]
- Bambie & Shawn's' boy George [1-year-old]

Bonnie and **Tawni** were always filling the air with music, singing and dance and the beauty of art, and they had been teaching the children a wide variety of songs and ways to express themselves in Art. Tawnies moving images were great fun for the little ones and the holographic image machine they brought with them were soon filled with images of fantasy and beauty. Bartlet had made a way to strum the cords on a device similar to the Lyrette by sitting at a keyboard and drums were made from tanned skins to accompany Bonnie's music.

Bartlet, Reece, and Bambie had become a formidable engineering team. They had designed and built a water filtration system, Heat generator, components for the chemistry and biology labs, and modifications to their weapons including a pretty good force field and weapons that even the children could use successfully, as half of their group was under 12 years old.

Mombo, Shepard, and Sadie had become organizer for the community collection and distribution of stores and manufacture of clothing. This would be a full-time job. Silos were built after the first harvest and they were separated in case, some marauders destroyed one. This group also made much of the food and bakery goods. Mombo turned out to be a great chef. He found rock salt and built an herb garden to support great tasting menus. Jothan had a number of seeds that help establish many of the foods including Mombo's garden.

Jothan and Maria had established the farming and produce details with each person in the community assigned to bringing in a certain amount of food during the week at harvest time. Already, new strains of wheat and corn were developed and a fast-growing fig tree was added to apple trees whose seed had been brought initially.

Jamma became the Village doctor and veterinarian to the 8 dogs, 12 deer-like animals, 3 horses, and 20 animals that were kin to sheep, probably 100 chickens, and 30 cattle. The cows were used for milk. Conrad was examining their DNA for some way to strengthen their herd.

Anne set up exercise programs for everyone including the children. Carla had helped her build a gym that was well used by the group. Anne helped in the farming as well. She certainly had a green thumb. Everything she stuck in the ground rooted.

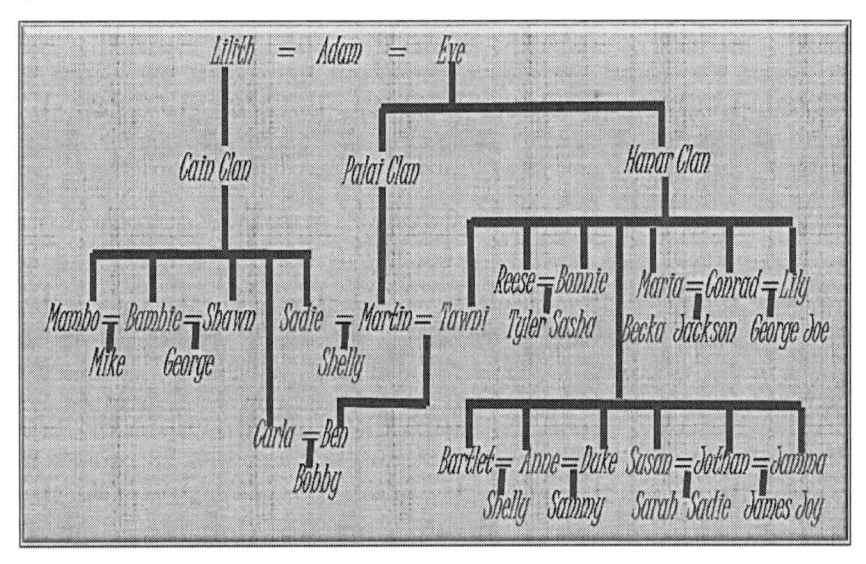

Conrad and Shawn headed up security with **Ben** in charge of the weapons. Unfortunately, strife between Shawn and Conrad was about to tear the group apart. Shawn believed he was the best leader because of he had been a highly decorated military officer and Conrad had just been in a lab. Conrad also became the Preacher of sorts and read from the books of Enoch and Noah often.

I arrived and I knew that Conrad had to hold the group together because of numbers, but right now preparations to hold onto their land had occupied their thoughts and strength. Shawn had established 2 different military groups with Conrad in command of one group and him in the other. Every other day, one group would have duty and from them the various watches were established.

There diligence was about to be challenged.

Attack

On the horizon were two M34 class ships and they were headed towards the community. The vehicles were mostly made for transport, but there was no telling what type of weapons and combatants were on board. The entire community went to a secure outcrop near the community. It wasn't a large cavern, but it was loaded with supplied and weapons that might be needed.

Soon the ships were directly above the town. No doubt this is what a group was doing; taking control of serfdom areas to help feed their communities and supply needed slaves. They were not going to win this battle. Conrad and Martin did their usual thing when I'm around. And they flew up to the ships invisibly and entered without issue. Conrad held onto Martin so he would know when to become visible. Inside the ship we were well hidden and saw a large army, possible 30 men, each with a firearm ready to subdue the farmers. We had taken with us, 'surprise bombs'. We placed three and left to find the second ship. We set our last bomb in that ship and quickly retreated.

Once on the ground, the first ship was hovering over the town looking for the 'soon to be victims'. With a loudspeaker, Jothan, said leave or be killed. We waited for a few minutes to see if they would decide to leave, but that was not an option. We detonated the first three bombs which caught the Cinnabar engines aflame and the ship became a ball of fire. The second ship still remained and a second warning was issued, but it seems anger weighed heavy on the intruders so that were almost to land when our single bomb blew their engine. Twelve soldiers appeared out of the blast 5 almost immediately fell into the massive spike pit that had been painfully dug. Now down to 7, the soldiers became more cautious and angry. Two reached a fence line and were immediately electrocuted. 5 more jumped the fence and entered the village proper but found no victims. It wasn't long before the last of the group spotted our outpost. Conrad and Martin got behind the group in their invisible way as a massive log rolled own on top of the remaining troops. Only 3 survived and Martin and Conrad, finished off the last of them. Not one of the homesteaders were harmed and new weapons and a substantial amount of other materials for the attacking ships was recovered. The group had used the simplest methods to produce a great victory. The remains of the attacking ships were left out in the open to be an ominous display to halt others who would want their beautiful land.

I knew, these people did not need me any longer. When I returned home, I tried to reattach to the ancient group again a year later, but the purse no longer worked as a corridor. It seems, I wasn't needed and therefore was not able to travel to them.

I was now home with this demon who loves hot sauce and a job I loved as well, but I had gotten used to the action.

Cindy said, *"That is quite a story."*

Without much of a pause, I told her something that I had learned a few days earlier, but I wasn't sure how to tell my new friend.

"Months ago, I wrote up an investigation plan and it has been accepted by the faculty. I will be going to one of the most famous sites of what is known as the Bharata War. I have received a grant to study the Anthropological significance of a place called Mohen jo Daro in southern Pakistan. My trip should take about a month."

There are so many artifacts in the area, I should have no problem finding a DNA link to understand these people and this important time.

She seemed sad that I was going and hurt that I was springing this on her like this.

Then I said, *"If you can take the time off, I would love for you to come with me."*

There are only 2 others who are anthropology majors who will be on my investigation team and I could use another set of eyes and you would be the prettiest investigator I could have.

Then she said, *"When would you be going--- or should I say when will you be investigating?"*

I said, *"In two months is the trip, after classes are out, I get my shots, and visa. As far as a time destination, it will be around 3200 BC."*

Cindy was just about as hooked on this time travel thing that was happening as me. She asked, *"What will I need to take?"*

I told her, *"Some clothes are all you will need as the University expects me to bring a writer. Besides, I certainly need my Therapist as weird as I have become."*

She said, *"I don't know why, but I'm in and you are right about being weird!"*

Jack said, *"I'm in, if anybody cares."*

Cindy then said, *"By the way, James is doing very well in school. We will have to help others."*

James, seemingly not being heard, said, *"I helped in that fixed fight you know!"*

I said, *"Please tell Jack you thank him for his effort in school."*

Cindy said, *"I'll do better than that,"* and she reached over and kissed me on the lips. *"How's that Jack?"*

Jack said, *"Can you do it again?"*

The next one was for me!

Considerations

I'm sorry my story is so filled with details outside my specific story, but I wanted you to understand my whole journey. I don't know how my Soul linked with this ancient DNA or whatever actually happened, but I know that something was guiding my journey as each time I returned it seemed to be when I was needed to be in place. My personal belief is that these guardian angels, you have heard about are somehow working to make our reality as perfect for us as possible. Once they found out about my empathy and cognitive soul thing, I have reasoned, they used it to get rid of wrinkles in time. Just think of me as an ironing board.

The trip back in time encouraged Noah for his important journey and helped save a supportable number of people from the kingdoms of Hanar, Palai, and Cain to assure diversification of the gene pool. This included helping secure their community from the onslaught of the Anak Giants which ensured that a wide assortment of ancient knowledge was supported. Lastly, I, somehow, reenergized the women of the Pleistocene. Don't ask me why these were necessary, but for some reason they were.

Ever since Einstein came up with his Relativity science that would make Time disappear when one travels or vibrates at what is laughingly called the "speed of light"; scientists have been scrambling to understand time and space better. The Quantum Physics of Neils Bohr has ripped time and space from everything, When Einstein was asked that common question, *"'If a tree falls in the woods and no one is around, does it make a sound?', Einstein and now all modern scientists say--- THERE IS NO TREE!"* Without a cognizant viewer, reality, space, and time don't exist. It is this fact of reality that ensures someone going the speed of light will never age. Somehow my soul is pulled backwards in time because there is no physical component. Other things to consider are following:

Time Travel-If we are to believe the evidence, the secret Rainbow Project and the Pegasus Project in the 1940s and 1950s both tested the time travel enigma without incident. Besides those projects, a large number of anomalous articles show that we have encountered some who came from the future to the past without any noticeable issue. I think pictures will help here. The following collage shows screen shots of three different movies from the early 20th century on the left potion of the collage. Each shows a person talking on a cell phone of some kind, well before anything like that was known. The bottom images were from a Charlie Chaplin movie that accidentally captured the 'Visitor' in the background. The image in the upper middle shows what looks like a surfer dude in a 1917 photograph. Below that, a Mohawk and tee shirt gives the traveler away.

The last image in the middle shows a seemingly impossible, modern, hoodie and tee-shirted, sunglasses wearing, visitor in 1930s picture. The large printed 'M' on the tee-shirt and his hoody are especially telling and unheard of by all the others wearing hats. The last column shows an of a watch effigy found in a 400-year-old Ming Dynasty tomb. To make this find stranger, the back is engraved with the word SWISS. Below that is a fossilized portion of a leg bone of an unfortunate traveler in a modern boot and the last shows a petrified 'modern' hat lost be someone.

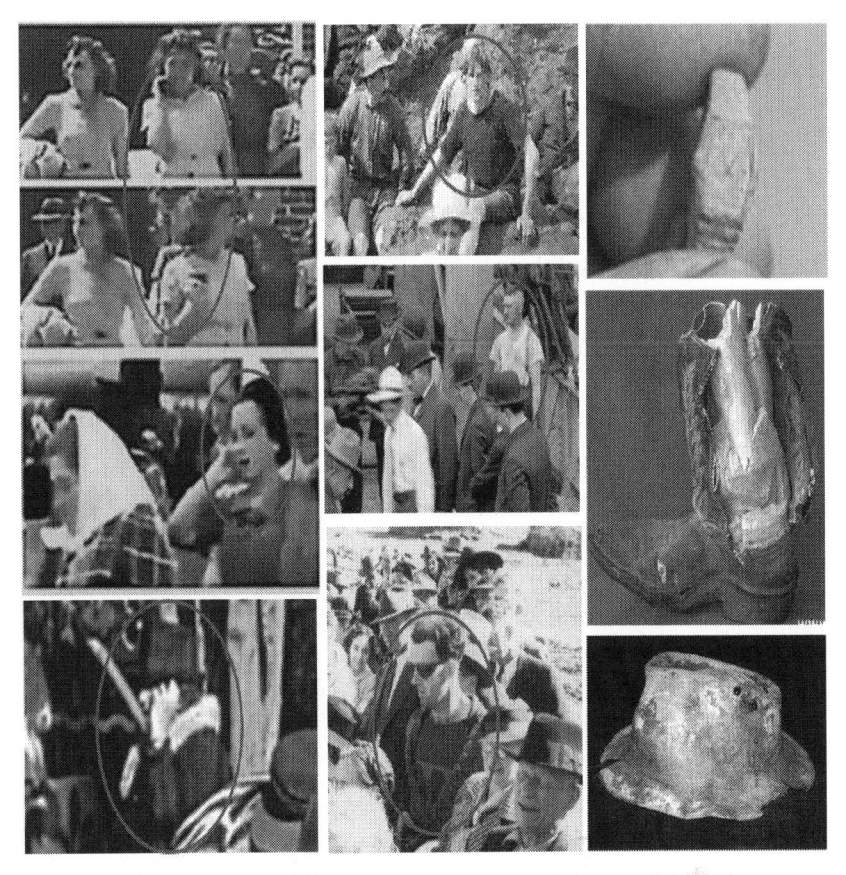

These all have one thing in common. They show images of people from the future. Also, half a dozen researchers from the Pegasus Project all told about time travel as a known capability even during the mid-20th century. One of the researchers was President Eisenhower's niece, to kind-of show a level of truth. Knowing time travel would not damage, regular time, was helpful, but I really had little control of my first time-exchange.

Pleistocene Societies-All a sudden, I was in the middle of the events that would result in the Pleistocene Extinction and nothing was going to stop the horror. What I could do is be responsible for saving a few of those who 'should have' survived. Seemingly impossible odds would be challenged and even matter itself had to be modified to allow for redemption and departure on a wild ride to safety. I needed to tell the story so I could understand all this, myself. I need you to know, so I can believe what happened and how it all happened. While finding out about myself, I also found out how to love those who would help me and those who needed my help, including a dead guy.

Many calling themselves scientists, continue to ignore thousands of pieces of evidence concerning the civilized people who lived during the Pleistocene, so I'm certain, some may have difficulty in understanding what had to be and how my travels affected those outcomes. That's where the ancient Jewish text, *"Generations of Adam"*, can help some more. This original version of this sacred book is believed to have been that used by Moses when he wrote chapter 5 of his book *"Genesis"* as it is fully described as the source and the details match the original.

> ***Genesis 5:1**- This is [from] the book "Generations of Adam". In the day that God created man, in the likeness of God made he him. --- Adam lived were nine hundred and thirty [jubilee] years--all the days of Seth were nine hundred and twelve [jubilee] years---Enos -Cainan -Mahalaleel-Jared -Mahalaleel- Jared -Enoch- Methuselah -Lamech-Noah.*

A short segment of this important history may help explain more about what I experienced than most of the 'pseudo'-history books and anthropological studies that are pushed on you as fact. I would even get a chance to meet some characters you have heard about named Methuselah, Lamech, and Noah. They absolutely are not fairy tale people. Besides establishing details about the first Adamic people, it also affirms some of the aspects of the Pleistocene Wars that are well established in the scientific record.

There are still a number of scientists who believe the eventual extinction of almost everything at the end of the Pleistocene, the earth shifting, and millions of giant mammoths very quickly becoming frozen solid are lies, but I got a unique opportunity to witness them first hand. We are told the Pleistocene people were established into at least 30 separate "Kingdoms" in the Eastern continent alone. I got a chance to interact with those from the Kingdoms of Shulon, Enoch, Palai, and Hanar and even see the great Anak people who lorded over many kingdoms and in some areas were worshipped as gods.

Who Were the Anak?

While the term Anak might seem strange, you may already know about them as they are also known as Nephilim, in Judeo-Christian histories. The Mongulala, in Brazil, called them the Akamim. In North America, they were called the Archaics. The Greek called them Olympians and the Dravidians of India called them the Arya. In Egypt, they were known as the Lords of Amenti, and the Sumerians called them Annunaki. Take your pick these people ruled over all the lands before and even after the Pleistocene Extinction. Anak lived longer than the Cro-Magnon so they ruled large groups of individual kingdoms like gods. When Anak people died, their souls were released, but unlike our souls, they are cursed to remain wandering outside of reality with no light, no comfort, no tasting, no sensations at all; only misery as something we call demons. The only way to relieve their horror is to possess humans or animals.

Causes of Destruction

The earth didn't just one day decide to destroy itself. It would take some time to cause the massive axis shift and I can tell you, dozens of texts from around the world, including 4 books of the Bible [*Psalms, Isaiah, Job, and Enoch*], described the destruction of the Planet Venus near the end of the Pleistocene, the destruction of one of the central commerce sites by flooding, and a massive shift in the Earth's axis all just before worldwide extinctions that ended the Pleistocene.

Hopefully, you are beginning to see a different image of the Pleistocene than the complete lie, established by those with blinders on. It was not a place where Neanderthal came around grunting and pulling on a female's hair or even a place where the Flintstones lived. Don't be confused by the limited artifacts as metalworks have completely rusted away. We still have ancient stories written down on stone, bones, artwork, and even details of the clothes these people wore. In my "travels", I found out the stories, images, and all the rest were more correct than anyone would think.

Only Two Races of People

Complex mapping of the human genome now shows, conclusively, by both Pairwise Nucleotide separation and number of differences that there are in DNA; there are only 2 major races of humans living today. This has been hidden to protect one group of people and to amplify the lies. The data is shown below. I know the Haplotype DNA mutation scientists have determined about 20 major races, but when the entire DNA stings are tested, the data is undeniable. I don't know what this means, but you can use the DNA mutation number or this one.

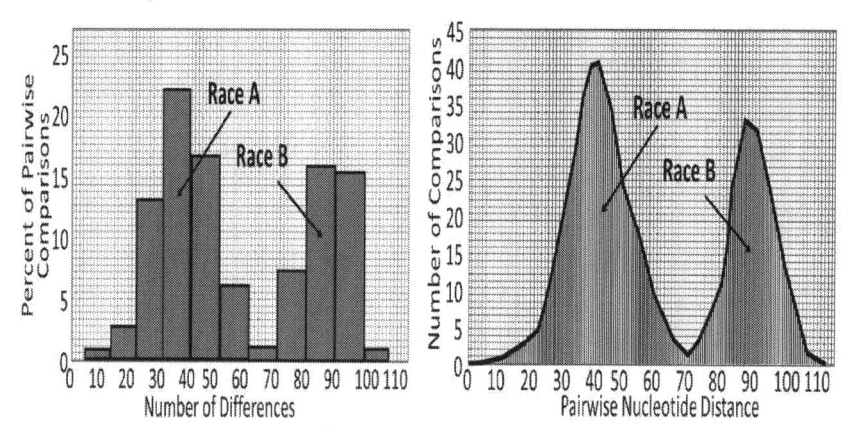

Instead of slope headed, hairy, barefooted animals, Neanderthal were red-headed and had tenor voices according to their DNA. They also had larger brains, did not grunt, and had sex with Cro-

Magnon. The signs of Neanderthal DNA so up more in South America than the rest of the world. Possibly I will study that later. Also, it is well known from DNA sequencing that Neanderthal people do not have African ancestors.

Pleistocene Wars

According to nuclear residue, mutations, melted walls, and many other things impossible to ignore, there were nuclear materials discharged during the warring during the last 1000 years of the Pleistocene that caused major mutations of humans. With hundreds of pieces of evidence, one would think this would be factored into our history, but all of it was simply ignored. Hopefully, my travels have helped some to understand details of this horrible time.

Unclean Animals

Ancient Geneticists developed all sorts of oddball animals called "unclean abominations" in biblical descriptions to separate those that had DNA modified and those that had actually been created by the Creator God. To keep from having to say ancient Geneticists were real, some go so far as to say most of the animals that our God created, he, for some unknown reason, hated—they were UNCLEAN to him. --- Pretty stupid. I was in close contact to one of many Pleistocene Genetic engineers making animals that God would later classify as "Unclean abominations".

Remade Dinosaurs

We know Pleistocene geneticists redeveloped dinosaurs about 20 thousand years ago because we are finding hundreds of dinosaur samples that are not fossilized. Some are trying to reconstruct wild methods to keep bone form fossilizing rather than admitting the most probable truth. While I did not see these dinosaurs, my engineer friend knew about and possibly help reestablish colonies of the Cretaceous animals during the Pleistocene.

Young Dryas Nuclear Fallout Fiasco

While there is absolutely no doubt that massive amounts of radiation "Happened" during the last part of the Pleistocene, in order to hide the wars, many try to say some Extraterrestrial event caused the younger Dryas without killing everything and then after it was done, almost everything died. This is pretty crazy and I hope my firsthand visit help you see the truth better.

Atlantis Lie

While there are many ancient texts from around the world describing the commerce- center known as Atlantis. There is little that suggests Atlantis was not real.

Demons

God's punishment of the millions of Angels who rebelled in the Heaven War is easily ignored by scientists who have never been infected by demonic possession, but thousands of people know all too well the misery of the group that is described over and over and over in our New Testament verses. Lucky for me, I came upon, or one was directed to me who wanted to know more truth and understood the lies he had been fed so many years.

I could go on and on about how quasi-scientist and those who call themselves ancient historians are destroying the truth. Parts of this story 'might be' made up, but it describes our past much better than the fiction put in the book described as scientific history.

In the next book, I will show how much they lied about the Bharata War. It was the worst worldwide war of our current Holocene Age. Ancient texts tell us that while the Pleistocene

Extinction certainly was more devastating to humanity, the Bharata War would kill 1/3 of the population around the world.

In the next book the J-man finds out more about his unusual gift, the world, demons, and his love.

With that I must end this book. Thanks for reading.

The End

About the Author

Steve Preston is a long lime author of scientific, esoteric facts. His books focus on the painful truths rather than whitewashed details that make us comfortable. If you are interested in the truth instead of comfort, please review other works by Mr. Preston as shown below. The images are some from Egypt with the writer taking the older version of taxi similar to what Moses might have used. To the right the writer is shown in the Jewish Negev desert of Israel where the Dead Sea Scrolls were found that were used by John the Baptist in his teachings and where copies of *"Generations of Adam"* were found.

His books include a wide assortment of different subjects including Biblical history and proofs, the story of man's development, Ancient technology, new views of Physics and Biology, and Ancient Wars. A partial list follows.

Development of Mankind

The First Creation of Man-book 1 History of mankind

The Second Creation of Man-book 2 History of mankind

The Creation of Adam and Eve-book 3 History of mankind

The Antediluvian War Years-book 4 History of mankind

Man After The Flood-book 5 History of mankind

A Closer Look at Ancient History-book 6 History of mankind

A New View of Modern History-book 7 History of mankind

The Twentieth Century and Beyond- Book 8 History of Mankind

Bible History, Correction, and Analysis

Abraham to Moses-First part of the Bible

Adam's First Wife-Story of Lilith

Adam to Abraham- Second Part of the Bible

Closer Look At Genesis- 200 ancient text confirm Genesis

Exploring Exodus- Reviewing the Details of "Exodus"

Errors in Understanding- Interpretations of the Bible

Expanded Genesis- Apocrypha and other Jewish texts

Exploring Genesis- Reviewing the details of "Genesis'

Incarnations of God- How often did God become Incarnated?

History Confirmed By The Bible- Science confirmation of the Bible

Moses Saved Egypt- How the Jews eliminated the Hyksos

Moses to Jesus- Third part of the Bible Series

Mysteries of the Exodus- Proofs of the Exodus

New look at the Bible- Questions in Interpretation

Old Testament Used By Jesus- Ancient Jewish texts

Understanding the New Testament-4th part of the Bible Series

Why the King James Bible Failed- Issues with KJB

Ancient Technology and Life

Ancient History of Flying- Ancient flying

Kingdoms Before the Flood- Pleistocene humans

Living on Venus- Venus before the Pleistocene Extinction

Martians- Ancient Life on Mars

Mysterious Pyramids- Who made the Pyramids?

Victory of the Earth- History of our Earth

Not from Space- UFOs are not from space.

Amazing Technology- Descriptions of prehistoric capabilities

Ancient and Modern War

America's Civil War Lie- Truth about the Civil War years

Behind the Tower of Babel- Story of the Bharata War

Driven Underground- Fear in the Bharata War

Four Armageddons- The 4 major wars that destroyed mankind

Six Deaths of Man- Destructions of mankind

World War Before- The Pleistocene War

World War with Heaven- The Angel and Nephilim War

World War Zero-The Bharata War

When Giants Ruled the Earth- History of the Titan Giants

Sex Crazed Angels- What caused the Heaven War?

Current Events and Fears

Allah' God of the Moon- Terror of Muslims
American School Disaster- fear in our country
Can We Save America? - Fear in the USA
Scythians Conquer Ireland- A History of Ireland
Fast History of MILES Training- Laser based Army training
Great American Quiz- Unusual details of American History
Make Your Own Global Warming
Truth About Phoenicia- The Evidence -First in America
Monsters are Alive- Post Pleistocene Monsters
Promote the General Welfare- Fear in USA
Our Very Odd Presidents- President review
Terror of Global Warming- Fake issue uncovered
The Antichrist- Many demonic possessed rulers
The Bad Side of Lincoln- Negative side of a great man
The Devil- Of Demons and their master
Vampires among Us- How Demons and Vampires are similar
Humans on Display- Slavery and Human Zoos

New Look at Physics
Amazing Technology- Pleistocene Technology
Anthropic Reality- We control our Reality
Consensus Science- Fake Science
Complex Earth- Truth behind Earth's development
Is Time Travel Possible? Science of Time Travel
Retiming the Earth- Eliminate of Nuclear Decay Errors

Releasing Your Consciousness- Beyond our SELF
Slip Through a Wall- How to walk through solids
Our 12-Dimensional Universe- New science of our Universe
Mystery of Photons and Light- Science of Photons
Of Heaven and Hell- scientific descriptions
Meaning of Life and Light- Detains of New Science
Vibrational Matter- New Science of Quantum Fluctuations

New Look at Biology
DNA of Our Ancestors- Tracing DNA of ancient man
God Didn't Make The Ape- New science on ape Evolution
Lizard People- Mutated People of the Bharata War
Creation and Death of Dinosaurs- Why Dinosaurs died
Races of Men- Tracing DNA of Humans
Tracing Cro-Magnon to Jesus- The third creation and mutation
Self, Soul, Spirit- Three components of Life
Self-Virtualization- New science of reality
True Happiness- Self Actualism and Beyond
Life Resonance- Unusual capabilities of men
Awaken the Departed- We can talk to the Dead
Biophotonics and Healing- How Photonics used in medicine

Made in the USA
Columbia, SC
08 June 2020